A VIEW TO A CHILL

PRAISE FOR LARISSA REINHART

The Finley Goodhart Crime Caper series

The Cupid Caper

"This is as fun a novel as it is moving and at times heart-breaking, never the more so when the final page comes and readers are only left wanting more." — Cynthia Chow, *King's River Life Magazine*

"Expertly written with engaging dialogue and a fast-paced read, this mystery kept me glued to the pages. Another great novel from Larissa and I look for more action with Fin, Lex and a surprise newcomer to their fold." — Dru Ann Love, Raven Award winning blogger at *Dru's Book Musings*

"Another great mystery by Larissa Reinhart. Con artists, murder, a cast of sinister characters, and some laughs along the way. Loved it." — Terri L. Austin, author of the *Rose Strickland Mysteries* and *Null For Hire* series.

———————

The Maizie Albright Star Detective Series

NC-17 (#3)

"The Maizie we meet at the beginning of this novel is not the woman who emerges at the end, and that is where the author excels. This is an undeniably fun mystery that makes the most of celebrity lifestyles and replacement of network television by streaming channels, yet never sacrifices character development for laughs." — Cynthia Chow, *Kings River Life Magazine*

"The mystery and detective cases drive the story, but Larissa Reinhart's characters steal the show every time." — The Girl with Book Lungs

"NC-17 is simply fabulous. Fans of cozy mysteries, southern chick lit, hick lit, crime capers, and humorous mysteries will love it." — Jane Reads

View To A Chill
(A Cherry Tucker & Maizie Albright novella)

"It was fun watching Maize and Cherry do what they do best, helping each other, indirectly, along the way in this engagingly entertaining drama. It was like having the best of both characters in the same story, yet separated by their roles. I look forward to more adventures together or separately with these lovable characters." — Dru Ann Love, Dru's Book Musing

"If you love southern settings with plenty of sweet tea and eccentric characters, the meet up of these two heroines is epic. Not only did I race through the pages, but I immediately download the first book in the series." — Barb Taub, humor writer and author of the *Null City* series

"If you love short mystery stories or novellas, this is the book for you." — Map Your Mystery

16 MILLIMETERS (# 2)

"Another fun outing for Maizie Albright, former child star. Larissa Reinhart always brings humor and grit to her mysteries." — Terri L. Austin, author of the *Rose Strickland Mysteries* and the *Null for Hire* series.

"The author so brilliantly creates an environment where Harvey Weinstein-like behavior could exist, and demonstrates how actresses must walk a delicate line in order to stay employed and still not be victimized. Maizie's missteps make each of her successes an absolute joy, and I encourage readers to delve into this lively, funny, and genuinely satisfying series." — Cynthia Chow, *Kings River Life Magazine*

"With visually descriptive narrative, humorous quips, witty repartee and a quirky cast of characters, this was a such a fun book to read. This was an engagingly entertaining book and I can't wait to see where we go next with Maize, Nash and the rest of the gang." — Dru Ann Love, Dru's Book Musing

15 MINUTES (#1)

"Larissa writes a delightful book. Suspense, romance, and some funny situations. [Maizie's] a teen star grown up to new possibilities." — Sharon Salituro, Fresh Fiction

"I love Larissa Reinhart's books because they are funny but they also show the big heart of the protagonist." —Lynn Farris, Hot Mystery Review

"Hollywood glitz meets backwoods grit in this fast-paced ride on D-list celeb Maizie Albright's waning star. Sassy, sexy, and fun, 15 Minutes is hours of enjoyment— and a wonderful start to a fun new series from the charmingly Southern-fried Reinhart." — Phoebe Fox, author of *The Breakup Doctor* series

"Maizie Albright is the kind of fresh, fun, and feisty 'star detective' I love spending time with, a kind of Nancy Drew meets Lucy Ricardo. Move over, Janet Evanovich. Reinhart is my new "star mystery writer!"— Penny Warner, author of *Death Of a Chocolate Cheater* and *The Code Busters Club*

"Child star and hilarious hot mess Maizie Albright trades Hollywood for the backwoods of Georgia and pure delight ensues. Maizie's my new favorite escape from reality." — Gretchen Archer, *USA Today* bestselling author of the *Davis Way Crime Caper* series

"This is a great start to a new series that boasts a quirky cast of characters, engaging dialogue and the liveliness that befits this delightfully amusing and fast-paced drama." — Dru Ann Love, *Dru's Book Musings*

The Cherry Tucker Mystery Series

A Composition In Murder (#6)

"Anytime artist Cherry Tucker has what she calls a Matlock moment, can investigating a murder be far behind? A Composition in Murder is a rollicking good time." – Terrie Farley Moran, Agatha Award-Winning Author of *Read to Death*

"Boasting a wonderful cast of characters, witty banter blooming with southern charm, this is a fantastic read and I especially love how this book ended with exciting new opportunities, making it one of the best book in this delightfully endearing series." — Dru Ann Love, *Dru's book musings*

"This is a winning series that continues to grow stronger and never fails to entertain with laughs, a little snark, and a ton of heart." – *Kings River Life Magazine*

The Body In The Landscape (#5)

"Cherry Tucker is a strong, sassy, Southern sleuth who keeps you on the edge of your seat. She's back in action in *The Body in the Landscape* with witty banter, Southern charm, plenty of suspects, and dead bodies—you will not be disappointed!" – Tonya Kappes, *USA Today* Bestselling Author

"Anyone who likes humorous mysteries will also enjoy local author Larissa Reinhart, who captures small town Georgia in the laugh- out-loud escapades of struggling artist Cherry Tucker." – *Fayette Woman Magazine*

"Portraits of freshly dead people turn up in strange places in Larissa Reinhart's mysteries, and her The Body in the Landscape is no exception. Because of Cherry's experiences, she knows that—Super Swine notwithstanding—man has always been the most dangerous game, making her the perfect protagonist for this giggle-inducing, down-home fun."— Betty Webb, *Mystery Scene Magazine*

Death In Perspective (#4)

"One fasten-your-seatbelt, pedal-to-the-metal mystery, and Cherry Tucker is the perfect sleuth to have behind the wheel. Smart, feisty, as tough as she is tender, Cherry's got justice in her crosshairs." – Tina Whittle, Author of the *Tai Randolph Mysteries*

"The perfect blend of funny, intriguing, and sexy! Another must-read masterpiece from the hilarious Cherry Tucker Mystery Series." – Ann Charles, *USA Today* Bestselling Author of the *Deadwood* and *Jackrabbit Junction Mystery Series*.

"Artist and accidental detective Cherry Tucker goes back to high school and finds plenty of trouble and skeletons...Reinhart's charming, sweet-tea flavored series keeps getting better!" – Gretchen Archer, *USA Today* Bestselling Author of the *Davis Way Crime Caper Series*

Hijack In Abstract (#3)

"The fast-paced plot careens through small-town politics and deadly rivalries, with zany side trips through art-world shenanigans and romantic hijinx. Like front-porch lemonade, Reinhart's cast of characters offer a perfect balance of tart and sweet." – Sophie Littlefield, Bestselling Author of *A Bad Day for Sorry*

"Reinhart manages to braid a complicated plot into a tight and funny tale. The reader grows to love Cherry and her quirky worldview, her sometimes misguided judgment, and the eccentric characters that populate the country of Halo, Georgia. Cozy fans will love this latest Cherry Tucker mystery."– Mary Marks, *New York Journal of Books*

"In HIJACK IN ABSTRACT, Cherry Tucker is back—tart-tongued and full of sass. With her paint-stained fingers in every pie, she's in for a truckload of trouble."– J.J. Murphy, Author of the *Algonquin Round Table Mysteries*

Still Life In Brunswick Stew (#2)

"Reinhart's country-fried mystery is as much fun as a ride on the tilt-a-whirl at a state fair. Her sleuth wields a paintbrush and unravels clues with equal skill and flair. Readers who like a little small-town charm with their mysteries will enjoy Reinhart's series." – Denise Swanson, *New York Times* Bestselling Author of the *Scumble River Mysteries*

"The hilariously droll Larissa Reinhart cooks up a quirky and entertaining page-turner! This charming mystery is delightfully Southern, surprisingly edgy, and deliciously unpredictable." – Hank Phillippi Ryan, Agatha Award-Winning Author of *Truth Be Told*

"This mystery keeps you laughing and guessing from the first page to the last. A whole-hearted five stars."– Denise Grover Swank, *New York Times* and *USA TODAY* bestselling author

"*Portrait of a Dead Guy* is an entertaining mystery full of quirky characters and solid plotting...Highly recommended for anyone who likes their mysteries strong and their mint juleps stronger!" – Jennie Bentley, *New York Times* Bestselling Author of *Flipped Out*

"Reinhart is a truly talented author and this book was one of the best cozy mysteries we reviewed this year." – *Mystery Tribune*

"It takes a rare talent to successfully portray a beer-and-hormone-addled artist as a sympathetic and worthy heroine, but Reinhart pulls it off with tongue-in-cheek panache. Cherry is a lovable riot, whether drooling over the town's hunky males, defending her dysfunctional family's honor, or snooping around murder scenes."— *Mystery Scene Magazine*

A VIEW TO A CHILL

A CHERRY TUCKER & MAIZIE ALBRIGHT
INTERCONNECTED MYSTERY

LARISSA REINHART

Past Perfect Press

A VIEW TO A CHILL

A Maizie Albright Star Detective and Cherry Tucker Mystery Novella

Previously published in THE 12 SLAYS OF CHRISTMAS (2017)

Copyright © 2018 by Larissa Reinhart

Author photograph by Scott Asano

Cover Design by The Killion Group, Inc.

ISBN: 978-1-7325298-9-2

Past Perfect Press

This is a work of fiction. Names, characters, places, and incidents are either the products of the author's imagination or are used fictitiously, and any resemblance to actual persons, living or dead, business establishments, events, or locales is purely coincidental.

Original Copyright © 2017 by Larissa Reinhart

Original Publication Date: December 4, 2017 in the anthology THE 12 SLAYS OF CHRISTMAS

Printed in the USA

BOOKS BY LARISSA REINHART

A Cherry Tucker Mystery Series

PORTRAIT OF A DEAD GUY (#1)

STILL LIFE IN BRUNSWICK STEW (#2)

HIJACK IN ABSTRACT (#3)

DEATH IN PERSPECTIVE (#4)

THE BODY IN THE LANDSCAPE (#5)

A VIEW TO A CHILL (#6)

A COMPOSITION IN MURDER (#7)

Novellas

A CHRISTMAS QUICK SKETCH in SLEIGH BELLS AND SLEUTHING
(box set)

THE VIGILANTE VIGNETTE

A MOTHERLODE OF TROUBLE

Audio

PORTRAIT OF A DEAD GUY

STILL LIFE IN BRUNSWICK STEW

Box Set

CHERRY TUCKER MYSTERIES 1-3

Maizie Albright Star Detective Series

15 MINUTES

16 MILLIMETERS

A VIEW TO A CHILL

NC-17

18 CALIBER

Box Set

#WANNABEDETECTIVE, MAIZIE ALBRIGHT 1-3

A Finley Goodhart Crime Caper Series

PIG'N A POKE (prequel, short story)

THE CUPID CAPER

Title TBA

For grandmothers everywhere. xoxo
And to the Hallmark Channel for entertaining me every Christmas.

1 MAIZIE ALBRIGHT

#LastChristmas(I'mGladIt'sNot)

WHO COULD TURN down a grandmother's request to find a missing granddaughter at Christmas? This is not a rhetorical question. The answer is Jolene Sweeney. Half-owner of Nash Security Solutions.

I'm Maizie Albright. I worked for the good half (as I call it) of Nash Security Solutions. To punish Wyatt Nash, as crazy ex-wives are wont to do, Jolene opened her own private investigation office. (She's competing against herself. Jolene's more into revenge than logic.) When a little, old lady — aka Celia Fowler — appealed to Jolene to help her find her granddaughter, Jolene estimated Mrs. Fowler's community and net worth and told Mrs. Fowler "Sweeney Security Solutions only deals with an exclusive clientele."

Too bad, so sad. A big no to finding her granddaughter. At Christmas, no less.

Besides acting as a pretender in the private eye world, Jolene's also a high-end real estate agent and a Who's Who in Black Pine society.

And nominated for Grinch of the year. By me.

Not just for turning down poor Mrs. Fowler. Jolene's one of the most spiteful women I'd met, and I recently moved to Black Pine from Hollywood, so that tells you something. Hollywood did spite for curtain calls. Jolene's spite would be lauded with an Oscar. Except it's not a performance. She had permanent RBF (resting bitch face) of the soul.

Enough of the dastardly Jolene Sweeney.

Who else would turn down a grandmother's request on Christmas? Wyatt Nash. My boss at Nash Security Solutions and the man of my dreams.

Wait, what? I meant it's the job of my dreams. After playing the lead in *Julie Pinkerton: Teen Detective*, I longed to be a real private investigator when I grew up. It just took me until age twenty-five to get there.

I digressed. Why would Nash turn down Mrs. Fowler? Nash did a good Southern gentleman. Normally he's concerned with the plight of the less fortunate. Not so big on helping the more fortunate, but we'd been burned by the more fortunate in recent investigations. My old therapist, Renata, would say he had a white knight complex. He also had a hard body, a wickedly sexy smile, and cool blue eyes, à la Paul Newman. Total PI McDishy. If you're into muscle-y men who rarely smiled (despite the sexiness) and created dictums against dating their subordinates.

Which evidently, I was.

Anyhoo, it seemed Mrs. Fowler was an oldy but a goody in the private investigation world of Black Pine—a world comprised of Nash Security Solutions and now Sweeney Security Solutions. Every Christmas for the last five years, Mrs. Fowler asked Nash to find her missing granddaughter. He obliged her the last four, but not this year.

"It's a wild goose chase," Nash had said. He took a turn from the front office, into his inner sanctum.

Maybe inner cubby would be a better definition. A smaller office comprised of a wooden desk, an ancient computer, and file cabinets holding Nash's wardrobe and surveillance gadgets. It smelled of old paper, dust, and a spicy, manly, pheromone-filled fragrance, I like to call Eau de Nash. When working reception and billing, I took yoga breaks to pull that scent into my lungs. It's like a scent hug from Nash.

Don't tell him. It sounds weird when I say it out loud.

Also, don't judge. Nash had a rule about hugging. He has way too many rules. Taking direction was in my wheelhouse, but the man needs to allow improv every once in a while.

On the other hand, the outer office, although dusty and run down, smelled like donuts. Nash Security Solutions is housed above Dixie Kreme Donuts in an old brick building on Black Pine's original main drag. Working for a private investigator housed in a donut shop was like an unrealized dream come true. Until my hips started to show the reality.

Nash strode back through the inner office door and stopped before the sagging couch where I sat. He's a pacer. Like a caged animal. But I'm not going there because it makes me want to pick up a stool and whip.

"Krystal Fowler doesn't want to be found," Nash continued. "At sixteen, she ran out on her no-account mother and has been running ever since. All I can ever tell her grandmother is Krystal's not reported dead or in prison. I can't do that again."

"Prison?" I gasped. "How can you be so cold-hearted?"

"Miss Albright, you need to toughen up if you want to be a private investigator. Krystal Fowler dropped out of school at sixteen. Her dad's been in prison most of her life. Meth addict mom. Krystal's been caught shoplifting numerous times and suspected of various other petty theft but was never charged. I talked to the local shop owners, and they said she was able to talk her way out of the arrests. Around here, she was considered something of a con artist. The most positive thing her neighbors and teachers had to say about Krystal Fowler is that they're surprised she's not in jail. Classic making of a felon. That's why I checked the prison records."

"But she's so young."

"It's tragic. But the bigger tragedy is what Krystal does to her grandmother. Poor Mrs. Fowler gets a call every year this time from Krystal with a sob story, asking for a handout. Mrs. Fowler wires her money and never hears from her until the next year. The girl is bleeding Mrs. Fowler dry, and I refuse to be a part of it any longer. I can not and will not take Mrs. Fowler's money. That girl is breaking her grandmother's heart."

I saw his logic. Mrs. Fowler was throwing away her money on finding Krystal.

Which is why I took on Mrs. Fowler's case for free. On personal time. Without telling Nash.

And now I drove a borrowed car (Thanks, Tiffany!) one hundred fifty miles away from Black Pine to Halo, Georgia—somewhere between Atlanta and Alabama—instead of spending my holiday in a cozy (surprising for five thousand square feet) cabin with my adorable, six-year-old, half-sister, Remi.

I had a day to get to Halo and back before Christmas Eve. Remington Marie Spayberry would not forgive me for missing the wait for Santa. Remi didn't care that I had a hot lead on Mrs. Fowler's granddaughter. Evidently, all those Christmas cartoons she'd been watching did not instill in her the generosity of the season. But then this was the first Christmas I got to spend with my sister in, like, ever. Before this year, Christmases were spent in tropical locations with my manager and mother, Vicki Albright. She likes the twofer of a getaway with our "Celebrities Best Holiday Destinations" appearance in magazines like *Hello!*, *InStyle*, and *People.*

Vicki didn't have anyone but me. Daddy had Remi and his wife, Carol Lynn. And all the extended Spayberrys in Black Pine, Georgia.

Except for this year. This Christmas, Vicki Albright had Giulio Belloni. I thought. Not exactly sure what's going on there and didn't want to know. Giulio had been my on-screen boyfriend on our reality show, *All is Albright.* I'd thought off-screen, too, until I left the show. His role was rewritten, by my manager — I mean mother — as her new paramour. (I know, ew.) Ratings. Anyway, they're in Fiji and I got to stay in Black Pine for Christmas.

Except I wasn't in Black Pine. I was in a whole other part of Georgia where Mrs. Fowler's sister lived. And unlike the dry and hazy gray North Georgia Mountains, west Georgia was windy, sleety, and freeze-y. I cranked the heater in Tiffany's Pontiac as high as it would go. I might have been born in Georgia, but I was raised in California. I was not cool with the cold. I mean, boots and sweaters were fun. But on my current salary (a pittance), I couldn't afford a last-minute, real winter coat. At least not one with natural fibers. Lucky for me, I already had boots and sweaters because we liked to pretend winter in Hollywood.

When I spoke with Mrs. Fowler at her home earlier that morning, she had said Krystal wanted money wired to Atlanta (natch) but had also asked her grandma about her great aunt's health. It'd made Mrs. Fowler hopeful that Krystal was interested in turning back to her roots.

I wasn't as skeptical as Nash, but I was also not stupid (despite the way my body makes me look).

"Does she have a relationship with your sister?" I had asked Mrs. Fowler. I followed her home after witnessing Nash's gentle yet disappointing rejection. She lived in a small, run-down ranch in a mid-century subdivision in Black Pine.

"No." Mrs. Fowler played with the edge of her Christmas sweater. "I barely saw Krystal. My sister saw her once or twice, I guess. Maybe at a family reunion and when she was born?"

"Why would Krystal be interested in her aunt?"

"They're family? It's Christmas." Mrs. Fowler blinked at me through her glasses.

I didn't think Christmas had anything to do with Krystal's interest in her aunt. "Do you have a picture of Krystal? Something current?"

While Mrs. Fowler hurried into another room, I took a stroll around her living room. The room was crammed with stuff.

Mainly boxes from QVC, Amazon, and eBay. Not many photographs. I happened upon a crystal sugar bowl full of gumdrops just before Mrs. Fowler returned. I crammed a wintergreen in my mouth and fast chewed.

"Here, Maizie." She handed me a photograph.

The picture showed a young girl. Dark-haired, oval faced, and pre-teen-ish. She wore cutoffs and a t-shirt, sitting crossarmed on the steps of a house. Looking aggrieved. I tried to imagine her older, less colt-ish, and less hostile. But then realized, after what Nash had told me, most likely, she was still antagonistic.

Or who knew. People changed. Maybe Nash couldn't find her because Krystal had become a nun. Like in *Sister Act*. My therapist Renata said to imagine the most positive outcome before focusing on the worst case scenario. Of course, almost-worst case scenario seems to happen to me a lot. But that's better than worst case, right?

"Do you have anything more recent?" I asked. "That's what I meant by current."

Mrs. Fowler shook her head. "I'm not good at remembering to take pictures. I was never sure when I'd see Krystal. Her mother wasn't reliable."

"Does Krystal know where your sister lived?"

"I think so. She's lived in the same house all her married life. Her husband's from Halo, Georgia."

"Did you tell your sister that Krystal might pay her a visit?"

Mrs. Fowler forehead crinkled. "No. Why would Krystal visit Martha Mae?"

Oh boy.

Mrs. Fowler paused. "You don't think Krystal intends to get money from my sister?"

I did think. But I patted Mrs. Fowler's hand and told her to call her sister. If Krystal hadn't already visited Martha Mae, Martha Mae might want to avoid her great-niece until we caught up with Krystal.

We meaning me since Nash had turned down the case.

I got the sister's address and phone number. "Tell Martha Mae I'm coming. If Krystal calls, have Martha Mae wait to invite her over until I get there. I'm going to talk to Krystal and see if I can get her to come back to Black Pine with me."

Mrs. Fowler threw her arms around me. She smelled like lavender and gumdrops. I hugged her back, pressing her bony body against my soft form. I probably smelled mostly of gumdrops.

"Maizie Albright," she whispered. "You're my Christmas angel. I know you'll get Krystal back."

Now, one hundred miles and several hours later, despite the icy rain descending on this part of Georgia, I still felt the warmth of that message. I intended to do my best to get this wayward granddaughter back into the loving arms of her grandmother. I'd do the same for any grandmother. It might take a miracle, but after all, it was Christmas.

2 CHERRY TUCKER

IN MY TWENTY-SIX YEARS, I'd experienced broken ribs, a bullet's grazing, and a goat hit-and-run. Add to that plenty of hangovers, food poisoning, and a bout of the chicken pox at age seven. But I'd never experienced the gut-aching, head-throbbing, bone-chilling misery that I'd felt since early this morning. Feeling puny, I'd skipped the Christmas sing-a-long with Todd's band at Red's County Line Tap the night before. Worse than puny. Tired, achy, and with a gnawing in my belly that wasn't hunger.

A big surprise, because I was always hungry.

"Cherry Tucker," my BFF Leah had said to me. "I can understand not wanting to hear Shawna Branson karaoke the 'Twelve Days of Christmas.' But if you don't even want to eat Red's turkey dinner, you best get yourself to bed."

And to her shock, I did.

Actually, I don't know who was more astonished: Leah, me, or the rest of my friends and family. They'd arrived at Red's for the second annual Christmas sing-a-long and found me missing. All my kin and kith were there except Grandpa Ed, who didn't do such silliness. And Deputy Luke Harper, who was working.

The weatherman promised an abominably icy Christmas,

unusual for our area, so all available deputies were on call. Our winters tend to be cool and dry for the most part. But send us one snowflake, and the town shuts down. We can't cope. Or drive. Luke had already broken up a fight in the Tru-Buy parking lot. It seemed there'd been a run on batteries, milk, and bread. Words were said. Which led to fists. And a pack of Pampers used as a weapon.

A first for Halo, Luke had said. He'd been left with diaper cleanup.

The next morning, I lay, staring at my painting, *Snug the Coonhound,* above my bed. Willing Snug to stop whirling. Snug was making my stomach cramp. Closing my eyes made it worse. I felt incapable of doing more than opening or closing my lids, but I was burning from the inside out. I eased back, pushing my warm, limp pillow with me until I could feel my bed's brass spindles cooling the back of my head. The chill tore through me like a two a.m. freight train. Trembling, I reached for the blanket I had recently kicked away.

Licking my parched lips, I wished Santa would put me out of my misery.

I needed some centering to stop the dizziness and stared out the window at the opposite wall. The previous night, I hadn't bothered to close my curtains. The lights from my neighbor's Christmas tree winked, reflecting on the window. I watched them dance and glow from across our short property divide, hoping their syncopation would bring me the focus to keep my stomach in check. Mrs. Boyes never bothered to shade her windows this time of year. She liked to share her Christmas spirit with her neighbors. Also, her fruitcake.

The thought of her fruitcake made me nauseous. And not just because Mrs. Boyes's fruitcake often had that effect. I refocused on the blinking lights.

Mrs. Boyes's living room was brightly lit against the gray and gloom hanging between our homes. Someone was sitting on the couch. I blinked, then narrowed my eyes. It looked like a reindeer sitting upright, legs crossed, and drinking from a mug. He wore a blue sweater, which seemed unnecessarily warm for an inside reindeer. I felt unnecessarily warm, but couldn't seem to stop watching him. Rain pattered against the window, causing the reflected Christmas lights to crystallize. The reindeer bent forward, its attention fixed on the window. Or the rain. Or maybe he saw me. Watching him from my bed.

A wave of fear flipped my stomach sideways.

"Don't be a fool," I said. "That reindeer can't see you. You've got no lights on." I turned my attention from the creepy reindeer. My stomach shifted back in place, and I heaved a sigh of relief.

I closed my eyes, opened them, and checked the window. The reindeer had disappeared. Wearing a blue sweater, Mrs. Boyes stood near the window, a package in hand. Probably ready to deposit it beneath the tree. My lids felt heavy, and my chin dipped to my chest. Rain pelted the window, lulling me to sleep.

My head jerked up. The rain had stopped. The Christmas lights continued to blink. And another figure emerged from behind the couch. Santa.

Had I slept my way to Christmas Eve? I licked my chapped lips, flexed my achy limbs, and wondered if these characters always appeared in flu-induced dreams. Maybe just at Christmas.

On this side of the room, Mrs. Boyes was gesturing to Santa. Her wild arm waves made me queasy. I had enjoyed her more as a reindeer, as disconcerting as that had been. At least the reindeer hadn't made sudden movements. And now Santa was approaching the reindeer.

Maybe he needed the reindeer to help with his sleigh?

No, Santa seemed to be talking to the reindeer. Calming her.

"Thank you, Santa," I whispered. "She'll give you cookies." Mrs. Boyes always had cookies. Unfortunately, the cookies were a better fit for skeet shoot practice than consumption. But she meant well.

At that thought, another bilious wave washed over me. I shut my eyes, waiting for the wave to crash. Rain splattered against the pane. I opened my eyes and refocused on the window, now oily with raindrops.

The reindeer pointed toward her front door and turned from Santa. Santa retraced his steps to the door and opened it. I struggled to keep my watch.

This odd Christmas special was wearing me out.

Movement caught my eye. Santa hadn't exited the door. He crept around the couch while Mrs. Boyes faced her tree.

She half-turned. Santa lunged. Grabbing a string of Christmas lights, Santa wrapped them around Mrs. Boyes's neck. She flailed against Santa. He jerked the light cord. Lights sparked and went out.

I jerked upright and leaned forward, fighting the vicious churning in my belly and the spots in my vision.

Her arms clawing at his suit, Mrs. Boyes slid down Santa's body. She yanked at his beard, ripping it sideways. Santa bent over her. And Mrs. Boyes disappeared beneath the window sill.

My head felt like it was going to explode. Heat scorched my neck. The churning in my stomach became a razor-sharp clawing I couldn't ignore. I rolled to the edge of the bed, slid to the floor, and crawled to the bathroom.

On my return, I dragged myself to the window and gripped the sides to stay upright. Leaning my perspiring forehead against the chilled glass, I searched the house next door. Once again, the Christmas lights blinked in syncopated rhythm on the tree. In my rectangular frame of reference, the living room was empty of people. A red blanket had been folded over the sofa's back. No reindeer. No Santa.

Sleet splattered against the roof and struck my window. Shivering, I lurched back to bed, burrowed beneath the blankets, and tried to make sense of what I saw. I had no idea how long I was in the bathroom. Unfortunately, I had passed out on the floor and woke up shaking from the cold. My room was dark. Maybe some trick of light since the bathroom had been so bright. Or maybe it was the rain. Or sleet. Or whatever was going on outside.

An icy gust rattled my pane. I shivered. Had I seen a crime or had it been a dream?

Unsettled, I pulled my sketchbook off the nightstand and drew Santa and the poor reindeer from memory. My recollection seemed clear despite the morbidly odd subject. My eyes grew hot and itchy, my body languorously heavy.

"I've got to report it," I muttered. "And I better do it now. I can't stay awake for nothing. Lord, help me. I don't know up from down."

Reaching outside the blankets and into the biting chill, I snatched my phone from the bedside table and stole it under the covers. I thumb dialed a number.

"I need to report an attempted murder," I mumbled. "I saw Santa strangling a reindeer."

#WinterNotSoWonderfulLand

SLEET PELTED the windows of Tiffany's Pontiac as I pulled off the slippery interstate and took the local highway into Halo. Halo's not a big town. On the outskirts are a few fast food places, an old Waffle Hut, and a Ford dealership. There's a train track that'll give you whiplash bumping over it and two boulevards that intersect into a kind of town square, which consisted of churches on each corner. Very old school Southern with bungalows, Victorian-type houses with deep porches, and some bigger homes that probably were once stately, but now appeared ragged around the edges.

Twenty-first century Mayberry. Kind of sad.

Black Pine would be like that if it wasn't a resort town with a lot of old money. And new money. The newest money being the film industry. Bad luck for an ex-celebrity who was told to stay away from the industry by a kind, yet firm judge in California. So hard to keep up with probation requirements when your reality show follows you to Georgia and stays because it's cheaper to film in Georgia than California. They're not allowed to film me.

Unless, apparently, I'm on the B-roll.

Martha Mae, Mrs. Fowler's sister, lived in one of the cottages leading away from the square, closer to the train tracks. It was a cute house squeezed between two other similarly-aged bungalows. Lights swayed from the porch, a big wreath hung on the door, and poinsettias lined the porch steps. The cottages on either side weren't as kept-up as Martha Mae's. It gladdened my heart to see someone caring so well for the historic home. It was probably as old as the tracks.

The poinsettias didn't look any happier than I did about the craptastic weather. I dodged icy raindrops that pelted my puffy Uniqulo jacket as I dashed from the curb to Martha Mae's porch. Slipping on the top step, I smacked a poinsettia with my boot, tipping the pot. I knelt to right the pot and placed it back in the saucer where a key lay. I guessed Martha Mae no longer kept her doors unlocked like small-town people used to do in the old days. But Martha Mae certainly didn't go to extreme lengths to keep her home protected from burglaries.

Nash would have had a field day with Martha Mae's lack of security. Most of our (few) jobs were security systems. The private investigation side of the business had taken a hit with two notorious cases we (I) had been (inadvertently) (sort-of inadvertently) involved in. Nash would have recommended trip alarms on the doors and windows with a keypad entry.

But then Martha Mae would have to key in her code every time a neighbor stopped by for coffee or a cup of sugar. She'd end up leaving the alarm off to simplify things. Ah, small-town life. Wouldn't it be nice to live in a place where everyone knew where you kept your key?

Or would it?

From her porch, I gazed out at the wet neighborhood where bright lights blinked from porches and gutters. Yards were decorated (including a humongous inflatable polar bear), and wreaths hung on the doors. Halo may not be glamorous, but it was cozy and safe. Black Pine wasn't much bigger, but the wealth invited greater vices and bigger crimes.

Which made me worry about Martha Mae. Krystal the con artist might take the sweet old lady for a ride. I turned back to the door and rang the bell. Rubbing my hands together, I waited and still getting no answer, knocked. Leaned out the porch and double checked that I had seen a car in the drive. Yep. A Buick LeSabre sedan. I wondered why she hadn't parked in the garage on a day like this.

Martha Mae's front windows were not shaded. I'd had some bad luck with peeping in windows and seeing things I shouldn't (a dead body for one), so I hesitated. Then peered into the picture window, shading my eyes with my mittened hands. Her tree blinked from the far corner of the room, gifts piled beneath. A sturdy couch and two wingback chairs surrounded a coffee table and faced, I presumed, a TV in the opposite corner from the tree. My heart stung, knowing Martha Mae was a widow with no children.

I'd have to wait until Martha Mae arrived to find out if I had missed Krystal. One thing I'd learned from Nash about sensitive information, it was better to get it in person. It's a lot harder to lie, skirt the truth, or hang up when you speak face-to-face.

Plus, I had driven all this way, and Martha Mae looked like the type who would have Christmas cookies on hand.

In the meantime, I figured I might as well continue the Peeping Tom routine. I crossed the porch to the smaller set of windows. Christmas window clings —snowflakes, angels, and snowmen — and lack of light kept me from seeing much. A dining room. Table not set for company.

Avoiding the slippery sidewalk, I crossed the wet grass to Tiffany's car waiting on the curb and slid inside. Huddled inside my coat, I pulled off my hat and shook out my damp hair, and used a tissue to blot the rain from my face. Rubbing my hands together, I gave myself over to warm thoughts.

Roasting chestnuts on an open fire. Yule logs. Tahiti.

Didn't help. I was wet and cold. I needed a hot shower, dry clothes, or at least a cup of coffee. Martha Mae's garage door was closed. Maybe the Buick was an extra car. Or a neighbor had picked her up. Martha Mae didn't have a cell phone, she had a landline.

Who didn't have a cell phone anymore? Besides me. Until Nash had given me the burner because couldn't afford a smartphone. Aha. Answered my own question.

I'd have to wait for Martha Mae's return. Wet, cold, and in need of coffee.

Near the highway, the Waffle Hut had looked enticing. The sign said they had a Christmas waffle. Red velvet with whipped cream cheese. More importantly, they had a bathroom with, hopefully, a hand dryer.

But what if Krystal showed while I was gone? Back in Black Pine, Mrs. Fowler's home phone didn't have a call log read-out. Her phone was attached to the wall with an actual cord. Avocado Green. Her sister probably had the same one in. Perhaps in harvest gold. So no phone number for Krystal. Google and social media hadn't revealed anything on the young woman either. She was off the grid.

I couldn't contact Krystal, yet Waffle Hut had red velvet waffles and hot coffee.

A dilemma.

I glanced at the house to the right of Martha Mae's. The cottage looked the most decrepit and the covered drive was filled with junk. It also wasn't decked out with Christmas decor like the others. An old yellow truck rested in the driveway, but it didn't look like it ran. The house was dark, and I assumed unoccupied. On the left, a cheerier cottage had a car in the drive and a Christmas tree in the front window. Also, the inflatable polar bear in the front yard.

I pulled on my wet hat and mittens (yuck), shot out of the car, and quick-stepped through the drizzle to the polar bear's front porch. A woman answered her door at my knock.

"Hello," I said. "My name is Maizie Albright. I'm waiting to talk to Martha Mae Boyes. She's not answering her door but is expecting me. Do you know where she went or when she'll be back?"

She squinted at me. "Maizie Albright?"

"Yes, ma'am."

"Did your parents name you after the actress?"

Considering the actress was me and born on the same day, I didn't know how to answer. "No. I'm Maizie Albright."

She smiled the smile of those speaking to the less intelligent. "Maybe you don't know her. Maizie Albright's an actress."

"I know her. I was named after myself. Because that's me. I live in Georgia now."

"Of course, you do, hon'." She nodded indulgently. "What did you need?"

"Martha Mae Boyes. Where is she?"

"Martha Mae doesn't buy anything. She's on a fixed income. We get a lot of solicitors this time of year. Are you selling windows or magazines?"

"I'm not selling anything." The sleety drizzle was turning into a soak. The raindrops smacked the edge of the porch and splattered. I took a step closer to the door. "I work for a private investigator in Black Pine. Martha Mae's sister is my client. She's expecting me. I need to talk to Martha Mae about her grand-niece."

"Martha Mae doesn't have a grand-niece." The lady began to shut her door. "I don't like the sound of this."

"I'm worried about Martha Mae—"

"Merry Christmas." The door shut.

I faced a wreath made of tiny Woodstocks surrounding Snoopy. Snoopy wore a Santa suit. "Snoopy, do investigators get coffee breaks? Nash didn't teach me that yet. But I really need one."

In answer, a rush of raw wind blew rain across the porch. I yelped and ran back to the car.

AT THE WAFFLE HUT, I ordered the Christmas special and a large coffee — extra hot — to go, then waited in line for the bathroom. The woman exiting the bathroom looked about as dry as I felt.

"Y'all go in, but the floor's a mess," she said. "They need to mop. This weather is just awful, isn't it? Supposed to get worse as the day gets on. You better get your shopping done and get home."

I nodded and smiled. Maybe that's where Martha Mae had gone. Shopping before the weather got worse. With hope in my heart that she'd be home soon, I entered the wet bathroom, skirted the muddy puddle, and hung my coat over the broken dryer. I dried off as best I could with paper towels and warm thoughts.

Red velvet waffles. Extra hot coffee. I mentally added sausage to my order.

Renata had taught me that you could make yourself happy from the outside in. Look good to feel good. Yanking off my soaked beanie, I shook it out in the sink and ruffled my wet hair, now darkened to auburn. I quickly parted and double-braided my hair.

And looked like Rebecca of Sunnybrook Farm after a weekend bender.

Wiping off my raccoon eyes, I touched up my mascara. My sea glass green eyes blinked back at me. Better. I sneezed. But I still looked cold, wet, and miserable.

Vicki, my manager (and mother), taught me that actresses should never reveal their inner misery because nobody really gave a shit. You were hired for a job. Do the job and be miserable on your own time. This was speaking to a fourteen-year-old who didn't want to work. She'd found out her daddy was remarrying and wanted to move home to Black Pine. Have a normal life. With normal Christmases.

But Mrs. Fowler needed my help. I wasn't fourteen. I was just wet and cold.

I cocked a hip, fixed a teenage sneer, and mustered up enough snark until I saw the character from my most famous role, Julia Pinkerton, staring back at me. This Julia Pinkerton didn't look fourteen, but she did have spunk. "Get over yourself, girl. You've gotta bust this case. I'll make it happen."

I never understood that line. The writers loved a catchphrase. But it worked.

Maybe it would for this case as well.

4 CHERRY TUCKER

I WOKE to find a hand covering my eyes. My body jerked, but I didn't have the strength to buck. I opened my mouth to scream, but could only muster a low howl.

The hand jerked off my eyes.

"What in the hell was that?" I recognized the voice of my sister, Casey. "Is she dying?"

My vision cleared. Grandpa Ed's woman, Pearl, loomed over me. She wore a concerned look and a Christmas sweatshirt. The sweatshirt had a pyramid of goats, each with an ornament hanging from its mouth. The kid on top held a star between its hooves.

"She's burning up with fever. Bet it's the flu." Pearl held her hand away from her sweatshirt. "I need to wash up. Don't want to get my goats sick with this. Looks ugly."

I moaned and rolled over, eyeing Casey's lean against the doorway. On a cold and wet December twenty-third, Casey wore a tank top, yoga pants, and flip-flops. In keeping with the season, the tank top read, "One of Santa's ho's." It was stretched over a rounded belly that didn't quite meet the top of the yoga pants.

"I'm sorry you're feeling so bad," said Casey. "But I don't want the baby sick, so I'm not coming in your room."

"You should go," I whimpered. "Let me die in peace."

"Who dies from the flu?" She rolled her eyes. Casey wasn't much of a history or science buff, but I could tell she was concerned. Enough that she'd brought Pearl to check on me. The sort-of step-grandparent we never wanted. "I made you chicken soup."

My parched mouth oozed drool, causing my stomach to roll. "No food talk. And stand still. You keep rockin', and it's making me nauseous."

"I'm not moving. I'll leave the soup in the—"

She backed into the kitchen until I returned from the bathroom. During that time, Pearl had stripped the bed, remade it, and placed an assortment of Gatorades on my nightstand.

Red, blue, and green. Christmasy. My stomach took another roll.

"Now then." Pearl placed a cool cloth on my head, tucked me into the hospital-cornered quilt, and squirted her hands with sanitizer. "What's all this about reporting a crime?"

I stared at my *Snug the Coonhound* painting above my bed. The last few hours were hazy. Snug was no help. He continued to undulate. "Ma'am?"

"Honey, you called the police. Beth Ann Simmons is filling in for Tamara and couldn't understand a word you said. Everyone knows you're sick, so they sent an ambulance over. Not an ambulance, really. That was needed with…well, never mind that. You don't need the details. The town is just a mess. And Line Creek has all their emergency people up on the interstate because of a pileup. Anyways, Sheriff Thompson sent June Peterson in her minivan in case you needed transport. But you didn't answer the door, so June went home. That's when she called Casey. Casey called your Grandpa Ed, and he sent me. Here we are."

"Good thing I'm not dying," I croaked. "I'd have to haunt June Peterson."

"Of course, you're not dying," said Pearl. "You just have the flu. Didn't you get a flu shot?"

"No, ma'am."

"Where's the sense the Lord gave you? Goodness knows I get a flu shot every year. I get one for the shingles, too. Now that's a disease you don't want to get."

I rolled, searching for a cool spot on my pillow. "I guess I'm lucky to only be dying from the flu then."

"Nonsense. Who dies from the flu? Now don't be calling 9-1-1 anymore. Leave the emergency responders to the real emergencies. You can call me. Or Casey, although she shouldn't come near you. I mean, look how she's dressed. Half her body is exposed to all sorts of germs not to mention the cold."

"I'm hotter than Hades, Pearl," said Casey. "I'd walk around in a bikini if I could get away with it in this town. I feel like I'm having a Kenmore electric range."

"She acts like she's the first person to ever experience pregnancy, I swear," whispered Pearl. "But still, she shouldn't risk it. Casey shouldn't be near this house. You don't even have a can of Lysol. People die from the flu, you know."

I opened my mouth, then closed it.

"Now I'm going to run to the store and get you some Lysol. Also, some Tylenol. Then I'm going to clean your bathroom. It's like you don't even know how to take care of yourself. You could have children by now, Cherry. And what will you do when those poor babies get sick without Lysol and Tylenol?"

I didn't have the energy to defend my mothering skills to imaginary sick children, so I lay back on the pillow and waited for her to leave. "Casey, you still here?"

She waddled into the doorway. "Yep."

"Did I really call 9-1-1?"

"Yep."

"Where's Luke?"

Her gaze circled the room and drifted down the hallway. "Busy. You know. Working."

"If I had called the sheriff's office, I know Luke would come. He said he'd check on me."

"With the weather and…and everything, the sheriff's office is hopping. It always is this time of year, you know that as well as anybody." Casey stroked her belly. "Just focus on resting and getting well. We'd all miss you if you couldn't come to Grandpa's on Christmas day. I'm making a turkey and—"

"No food." I rolled onto my back and panted. Snug panted with me. "I kind of remember calling 9-1-1 now."

Casey turned in the doorway to face me. "What'd you tell Ann? Uncle Will said it was gibberish. He's worried about you."

"I thought I saw—" I rubbed my head, slid to ease against the bedstead, and checked Mrs. Boyes's window. In the corner, reflected lights from the tree blinked. Her living room was dark, but I could see a glow in the back of the house. "I don't know what I saw. Mrs. Boyes next door. Remember her?" I pointed toward the window.

"Yeah, sure." Casey glanced in the direction of my point.

"I was watching her through the windows. You can see straight into her living room. She looked like a reindeer, but never mind that. I think the flu's messed my brain. She had a visitor. Santa."

"Santa?" Casey snorted. "He's got one more day until he shows."

"And I thought Mrs. Boyes and Santa were arguing. Except she was a reindeer. And then Santa left. But he came back and strangled her with the Christmas lights."

Hugging her belly, Casey doubled over with laughter.

"I know," I said. "I don't believe it either. But Casey, it looked as real as you. Except it was raining. And kind of blurry. And…I don't know what I saw."

"So, you reported it anyway." Casey rolled her eyes. "Only you would report a crime on her deathbed."

I slid under the covers. "I thought you said no one dies from the flu."

"Not healthy young folks like you."

"I'm not healthy," I whimpered. "I have the flu. And I feel like death."

"Better than Mrs. Boyes felt getting strangled by a reindeer." Casey snorted.

"Santa," I whispered. "She was the reindeer."

Casey crossed the room to peer out the window. "You want me to go check on her?"

I stared at Snug. He still made me dizzy. Maybe I shouldn't have painted the coon dog in cerise and tangerine and stuck to browns. I swung my gaze to Casey. "Yes, I guess I do."

"You got any cookies to bring her? I need to have some reason to knock other than asking her if Santa visited early."

I double blinked at the word cookies and felt my stomach bubble into my throat. I rolled onto my side, slid out of bed, and crept to the bathroom.

"Never mind," called Casey. "I'll see you in a minute."

WHEN I RETURNED from the bathroom, the room was empty and dark. I turned on the light, crept back into bed, and huddled beneath the heavy quilt. My eyes crept to the window. Mrs. Boyes's overhead living room light flashed on. Remembering Casey's mission, I forced myself to sit up and focus.

A man was crossing through the living room from the back hall. He wore a white t-shirt. No Santa suit. I sighed and rested my chin on my knees. The man opened the front door, and after a long pause, Casey shuffled into the living room. She'd pulled a knit hat over her long, dark hair and covered up with a jacket, but left it hanging open. She glanced around the living room as she talked. The man waved at the back hall entrance.

After a moment, Casey nodded. She spoke, then waved to the window.

The man turned toward the window and also waved.

Realizing my lights were now on, I held up a hand and let it drop.

Casey turned toward the hall once more, spoke, then exited the house.

As the front door shut behind her, the man in the white t-shirt sauntered to the window facing my bedroom. Placing his hands on his hips, he stared for a moment. Covering his eyes, he leaned against the pane. He was older. Gray seasoned his thick hair and beard, maybe giving my flu-addled brain the impression of Santa. He didn't have Santa's build, though. With his arm flexed, his forearms and shoulders bulged. No bowl full of jelly either.

The man squinted through the dark. Might've met my eyes, although it was difficult to tell through the rain and gloom filling the small space between our houses. Not-Santa grinned and waved once more.

His grin showed in his teeth but not in his narrowed eyes. Definitely not Santa.

I shivered and slunk lower into my quilt. Reached for my sketchbook and a pencil on the nightstand. Then drew a quick sketch of the man in Mrs. Boyes's living room.

5 MAIZIE ALBRIGHT

#OMGDidHeJustSay #PleaseComeHomeForChristmas

RED VELVET WAFFLES are difficult to eat in a car. I don't recommend it. Particularly with a plastic spork and mittens. However, the hot coffee did the trick. I revived. Damp instead of drenched. Tiffany's car had smelled like wet boots and pine tree freshener, but now the wet pine boots had mixed with sweet waffles and coffee.

Wet pine coffee waffles. A definite improvement.

I sat across the street from Martha Mae's semi-dark house, waiting for her return. Feeling moderately cheery about my stakeout. It was about time I did some real investigative work. Although this field experience — like my past fieldwork — was not on Nash Security Solutions's docket. I wasn't sure if it counted as real. One of these days — I hoped. Prayed. Wished — Nash and I would do for-real fieldwork together.

I took a minute to dream about those possibilities, leading me down an imaginary road (we weren't supposed to take) that involved a lot of heavy lip action between the blue-eyed PI and myself. I'd gotten a taste. Once. And it was sweeter than red velvet waffle. And that red velvet waffle had made my teeth itch. Unfortunately, the romantic detour Nash and I'd taken had been short. Brief. Temporary. Fleeting.

Unfortunately, I hadn't been the one who'd fled.

Although the memory was warming me up — silver lining there — I forced myself to stop thinking about Nash. The temperature was plummeting. And with the icy rain, I worried about Martha Mae out in this nasty weather. She was of hip-breaking age.

As I waited, vehicles pulled into the neighbors' drives. An old Firebird and a big truck stopped at the house I thought was abandoned. Two women exited the vehicles, hurried into the carport, and through a side door. The house blazed with light. Across the street, an old Cadillac pulled into the drive of a rambling Victorian. An older man disappeared into that house, and a string of blinking, colored lights lit up his porch. I sipped coffee and watched Martha Mae's house.

Nothing happened.

Except for more sleet. Wind. My waffle was gone (I had better luck using my hands). And I now had to pee.

But — I reminded myself — this was my dream job. I was investigating a missing person's case. An actual granddaughter. Who might be a felon. But she might also be a nun. Life was funny like that.

Sleet pelted the car. I sipped more coffee. Turned on the radio and sang along to "Baby It's Cold Outside" (both parts) while I watched the big truck leave the neighbor's house. Did my Marilyn imitation singing "Santa Baby" complete with shoulder shrugs in my imaginary mink.

"Have A Holly Jolly Christmas" came on. I took a coffee break. A phone rang. I jerked. Coffee missed my mouth and rained on my puffy coat. My phone. I'd almost forgotten.

I had given up my smartphone when I left California (mainly so my manager/mother couldn't find me). Nash had given me a burner phone. It was rarely used (unless my manager/mother was trying to find me.) But I loved the little flip that couldn't do anything but make calls and take grainy pictures. I checked the screen. Nash. I grinned.

Wait, a minute. Nash didn't know I had taken on Mrs. Fowler's case.

My hello was tentative at best.

"Where are you?" said Nash.

"Out of town? It's very seasonal here."

"And here is?"

"Not like seasonal snow," I continued, astutely avoiding his question. "But it's cold. And wet. So more seasonal than I was used to in California. But I can't say it's a white Christmas."

"I'm not asking for a weather report, Miss Albright. I'm asking for a location."

"I'm still in Georgia. Which is why the seasonal weather surprised me."

"Please don't tell me you drove your scooter out of town."

"Lucky's a dirt bike, but no. My thighs couldn't take that long of a drive. I borrowed Tiffany's car."

"Your thighs—" He cleared his throat. "How long of a drive? Where are you?"

"A little town called Halo."

A figure emerged from the neighbor's house and walked across the driveway. A woman wearing an unzipped jacket, flip-flops, and hat.

Who wears flip-flops in sleet? Was this sleet? Not really rain, not really ice, definitely not snow. I shivered.

"You're helping Mrs. Fowler," said Nash.

"I'm not taking her money. She already wired some to Krystal. I know you felt guilty about taking her money."

"So, you're helping her for free." He sighed. "Miss Albright."

"I know. Merry Christmas."

"Where did Mrs. Fowler send you?"

"To her sister, Martha Mae's, house. Krystal had asked about her. I thought it'd be helpful for me to come down here and see if Krystal shows."

"And did she?"

"Not yet. I don't think."

"Are you with Martha Mae right now? Did you talk to her?"

"Not exactly. Martha Mae's not home yet. I'm waiting." I bounced on the seat. "I'm keeping surveillance on her house. And since we're speaking of surveillance, you know mentor to mentee...am I a mentee? That doesn't sound right. Mentoree? Anyway, how many coffee breaks do you usually take when on a stakeout?"

His second sigh was longer. And very audible.

"Miss Albright, come home. And please drive carefully. The weather is supposed to get worse."

"What if Krystal shows up?"

"Krystal Fowler was arrested three days ago. She's not going to show."

"Oh." Why did I find that disappointing? I had really hoped she'd become a nun.

But hold on. "Wait a minute," I said. "That means you've been looking at arrest records. You're also helping Mrs. Fowler. For free."

"Merry Christmas."

"Busted." My heart flip-flopped. Nash was no Grinch. I knew it all along. "Why were you looking for me anyway?"

"I wanted to—" He was silent for a moment.

I gave him the moment. Across the street, the woman in flip-flops, looking very pregnant — What was she thinking? She could slip and fall in flip-flops. Plus weren't wet, cold feet bad for your health? I shouldn't judge. But here I was judging — had marched from the neighbor's house to Martha Mae's. In the sleet.

I almost leaned out my window to tell the semi-barefoot, pregnant woman that Martha Mae wasn't home and to warm her feet back inside her house.

But Martha Mae's living room lit up. The door opened for the pregnant woman.

Shizzles, I thought. I should have rung again instead of assuming Martha Mae wasn't home. Where was my common sense? I studied the parked car, trying to understand how I missed her. Hells. Had the Buick moved? I couldn't tell.

An older man had opened Martha Mae's door. The pregnant woman went inside. Scooting closer to the front windshield, I craned my neck to watch them through Martha Mae's living room window. My vantage point in Tiffany's car made it almost impossible to see anything. Two shapes backlit by blinking Christmas tree lights.

Who was the man? Mrs. Fowler's had said Martha Mae's husband had died. Martha Mae didn't have children. Was he home when I rang? If he was, why wouldn't he answer for me? Because I wasn't from Halo?

This town was a little odd.

"And anyway…"

Craptastic, Nash had been speaking and I had forgotten to listen. I could usually multi-task. Why didn't I tune in for Nash of all people?

"It's Christmas," he continued. "So, I thought it'd be nice."

"Oh." My eyes flicked back to Martha Mae's house. What was nice? Christmas?

"If you don't want to because of our situation, I understand," said Nash. "Did you already make Christmas Eve plans with Mowry? Or someone else?"

Wait, what?

"Plans?" Plans sounded like a date. Did Nash ask me out on a date when I wasn't listening? How could I have stopped listening? But he said no dating until our two-year apprenticeship was up. And he didn't actually use the word "dating." Maybe there was a Christmas loophole. What a time to focus on work instead of my love life.

Shizzles, that's not what I meant.

I opened my mouth to speak, but couldn't find the words that wouldn't make me sound like a desperate nut job.

"I'll let you think about it," said Nash.

And lost my opportunity.

"Call me when you get back. Drive safe."

He'd hung up. I stared at the phone. Switched to Martha Mae's house. The pregnant woman was leaving, walking back across Martha Mae's yard. Should I call Nash back? Drive home?

But who was the man in Martha Mae's house? It'd only take a moment to find out. Maybe he would know if Krystal had called or talked to Martha Mae. But wait, she'd been arrested three days ago. When did Mrs. Fowler talk to her?

Before she was arrested? If so, must've been just before. So, no way Krystal had contacted Martha Mae. Unless... Did Nash check to see if Krystal had gotten out on bail? When I'd been arrested (Fiancé-Accessory Before the Fact), I'd only been in jail for a day before my initial appearance with the judge. She could have posted bail. We didn't know anything about Krystal.

Although I no longer believed she could be a nun.

Best to not assume anything, I thought. Just in case. Look what happened when I assumed Martha Mae wasn't home. A man had been there. Maybe he was a house sitter. And what if Krystal does get out on bail? I should probably warn Martha Mae that Krystal had been interested in her health.

In answer to my good Samaritanism, the sky opened. The icy drizzle turned into a downpour. I crawled into the backseat of Tiffany's car where she had a variety of miscellaneous goods. I flipped through the debris. Tampons. Mascara. Lotion. Nail polish. Hallelujah, an umbrella. Cracking open the door, I shoved the umbrella toward the sky and opened it. Three spokes were bent, but a half-working umbrella was better than none.

I took a step into the street, slipped, and grabbed the door. Steadied myself as the sleet rained into the car. (What Tiffany did not have in her car was a towel.) Shoved the car door closed, turned (carefully), and shimmied across the road. The umbrella protected my face. My back, however, was soaked by the time I made it onto Martha Mae's porch. Shaking off the umbrella, I set it to the side and prepared my "I'm not wet and cold but happy to meet you" face. It used to be my promo face. Very useful when you do thirty back-to-back interviews during a release.

Past acting experience can be useful when applied discriminately.

The older, bearded man opened the door halfway. "Yes?"

"I'm Maizie Al—" That hadn't worked well with Martha Mae's neighbor. I tried again. "I'm Maizie, and I work for Martha Mae's sister, Celia Fowler, up in Black Pine. Are you a relative of Martha Mae?"

"Why?" His eyebrows knitted and lowered.

Small town people were a lot more suspicious than I imagined. I thought they'd be more open and trusting, offering me cookies and gossip. Like in The Hallmark Channel's small-town movies. What was up with Halo?

"Mrs. Fowler's granddaughter, Krystal, may try to contact Martha Mae. I wanted to speak to Martha Mae. Is she home?"

"She's resting."

"I see. Did she do a lot of shopping today? With this weather, the shopping must have worn her out." I forced a hearty chuckle. But fell flat. He was not amused. "Can I get your name?"

His gaze shifted behind me.

I glanced over my shoulder but didn't see anything.

"What do you know about Krystal?" he said.

"Are you related? Because I'm—"

"Distantly," he said. "But I know Krystal and Celia Fowler. You can speak plainly."

I wasn't sure if I could speak plainly. I had a flashback to an early *Julia Pinkerton: Teen Detective* episode. Julia's basketball-star boyfriend was involved in a drug ring. She had snuck into the boys' locker room looking for him. His friend, Will, asked more questions than answered. Julia took that as a tipoff and learned

Will had been double-crossing Xavier. This man seemed as suspicious as Will.

"Your name wouldn't be Will, by chance?" I gave him my *Covergirl* smile — girl-next-door friendly — hoping to relax him.

He shook his head. "No. Are you looking for a Will, too?"

"Not really." Broadening my smile, my teeth gleamed (I hoped) in the porch Christmas lights. The lights not yet frosted in a coating of ice. "Have you heard from Krystal?"

No reaction from Not-Will.

I rubbed my arms and blew on my mittens. "I'm super cold. Could I come in for a minute?"

Not-Will considered, then opened the door. "Just for a minute. Martha Mae is resting."

"Of course." I quick-stepped past Not-Will, took a fast gander around the living room, and slid a few steps toward the doorway into the hall. "So, Martha Mae's sleeping?"

"Did the gal next door send you?"

"The pregnant one?" I considered his question and took another step back toward the hall. "No. I just saw her leave. Mrs. Fowler sent me."

"But you know the gal next door. The sick one."

"I'm sorry I don't." I half-turned and glanced down the hallway. Light shone through the cracks around the door in a room at the end of the hall. "I'm from Black Pine, not Halo. That's where Mrs. Fowler lives. Anyhoo, could you check to see if Martha Mae is awake? I'd really appreciate it. I'd like to drive home before the weather gets any worse."

He nodded. "Why don't you check out the tree while you wait?"

Odd request but okay. Maybe he or Martha Mae was super proud of their tree decorating abilities. I wandered to the tree in the far corner of the room, glanced at the colored balls and bubble lights. Spun around.

Not-Will stood right behind me.

I hopped back, bumping the Christmas tree. The tree shook,

splashing colored light across his face.

"I thought you were checking on Martha Mae? Tell her I only need to talk a few minutes."

The man nodded and retreated to the hall. He needed a lesson in personal space. Also in creepy house guest behavior.

A door creaked. The man returned.

"Martha Mae's real tired," he said. "She's sleeping. She don't have nothing to do with Krystal anyway. Hasn't seen her in years. But maybe I can help. Have you seen Krystal recently? Her family'd really like to know where she's been keeping herself."

"Me, personally? No. Mrs. Fowler has been looking for Krystal for five years. So sad." I didn't feel comfortable adding our recent news about her arrest. If he were family, he'd find out soon enough. "How are you related to Krystal?"

He shrugged. "Blood's blood. Just about everyone is related in these parts."

Probably true. "And I already forgot your name. What was it again?" Because you didn't tell me in the first place.

"Jay." He folded his arms. "You need to get back to Black Pine. The weather's turning."

"I thought it already turned." I chuckled, and getting me no reaction, handed him a Nash Security Solutions card. " If you see or hear from Krystal, can you call me? Please share it with Martha Mae, too. Krystal may be in some trouble, and Mrs. Fowler thought she might turn up in Halo."

"Why's that?" he said. "Krystal's never lived in Halo."

"Krystal asked about Martha Mae."

"Did she now?" He rocked back on his heels.

"Um, yes. Mrs. Fowler really just wants to see Krystal. She's worried about her. It's been five years and—"

"Celia Fowler don't care nothing about Krystal. She didn't take her in when Krystal needed her. She's the reason Krystal is in trouble now." Jay shoved me toward the door. "Now get yourself outta this house and don't come back."

6 CHERRY TUCKER

MRS. BOYES'S living room remained lit. I watched Not-Santa's blurry form retreat to the back hall and disappear. The overhead gleam of her living room, spangled with the blinking tree lights, shone against the gloom that had descended between our homes. In comparison, my bedroom felt cold and starkly lit. If Luke ever got off work, I thought, it'd be nice to sit in that warm glow with him. Even if I was sick.

When Casey returned, I asked for a string of Christmas lights. If she could find a spare.

"You want a what?" said Casey. "You hate Christmas decorations. You're feverish."

"Maybe so," I said. "But I can't get warm, and I thought..."

I didn't know what I thought. I just wanted a string of lights. And could no longer remember why. "Maybe I am feverish."

"We'll assume so. I ain't going to touch you. Lie down and stop watching Mrs. Boyes's house. It's making you crazy."

"It's the flu."

"But now that you mention it," said Casey. "This house needs a few Christmas touches."

"No."

"You're real sick, and I don't see you making it to the farm on

Christmas day. We'll come here. Therefore, we need to bring Christmas with us."

"You know I don't do Christmas."

"You give gifts. You go to church with us. You definitely eat my Christmas dinner every year. That's doing Christmas, ain't it?"

I groaned. "Please don't mention Christmas dinner. I was going to bring Luke to the farm this year. If his family will let him go. But I guess not anymore."

"Put that out of your mind." Casey rubbed her arms. "Just plan on us coming here. I'll take care of everything. But I ain't cooking Christmas dinner without Grandma Jo's Christmas china. And a few other things. You're just going to have to put up with a little Christmas in your house this year."

"No more talk about cooking. Who was that man next door?"

"Mrs. Boyes's nephew. He's visiting her for Christmas. She's fine. Slipped. She's flat on her back."

"You saw her?"

"She was sleeping. Anyway, she can't get up." Casey stretched and rubbed her belly. "I'm having the same problem lately. Nik has to pull me out of bed. Also out of Mr. Max's hot tub. But that was worth it—"

"You're going to make me sick again."

"All this talk makes me want to call Nik. And I need to check on…something," said Casey. "You rest."

Casey left and I turned my attention to the window. Sleet pounded the tin roof and frosted the edges of my window. I let the rain lull me for a moment, but blinked at movement in the house next door. The nephew had reappeared from the back hall and strode across the living room.

I glanced toward my bedroom door, heard Casey's murmur, and turned my attention back to Mrs. Boyes's house.

He'd opened the door partially, blocking my view. A minute or two passed, the door widened, and a young woman walked in. She wore expensive looking knee-high boots, jeans, and a puffy silver coat. Looked like she'd gotten the worse end of the weather. Long, red braids plastered to her jacket. She didn't look like Halo, although she looked vaguely familiar. Hard to tell through the wavy glass of our wet windows. She had that long-legged model way of walking that didn't match the heavy, country trod of folks around here.

While she talked — and her mouth didn't seem to close — the woman openly looked around the room and peeked into the hallway. Pretty brazen for a guest, at least in my neck of the woods. With that swishy walk of hers, she moved toward the tree, and I got a better look. Even drenched like a drowned rat, she was pretty. More than pretty, if I was honest. Not Shawna Branson-pretty, either. Too pretty for Halo, that was for damn sure. Not the kind of beauty I liked to paint, though. Her features were more suited for a camera lens than a painter's canvas.

Maybe the flu was making me catty. But what was someone like her doing in Mrs. Boyes's house? Looking around like that?

The nephew had crossed the living room in three, quick strides to stand behind the woman. Sweat broke out on my forehead and my hands clenched. Hadn't this happened before? Santa and the reindeer? My heart sped up. I hollered at the woman. Stupidly. She couldn't hear me. I could barely hear me. My throat was parched, so my voice barely rose above a hoarse, exaggerated whisper.

Before the nephew reached for the tree lights, the out-of-towner pivoted and found herself eyeball-to-eyeball with the man. I couldn't see her reaction, but she backed into the tree making the lights shudder and flicker.

My stomach rolled, kicked my other organs to the side, and crawled up my throat. I made a quick passage to the bathroom.

When I returned, the beauty was gone. I added the movie star to my sketchbook and flipped back through the drawings, trying to sort the oddness in the house next door.

#Everybody'sWaitingForTheMenWithTheBags

IN THE WAFFLE HUT, I held a fresh cup of coffee. And (if you want to get technical) I ordered another red velvet waffle. I told myself I was preparing for the drive back to the mountains. I was also piecing together what I knew.

Mrs. Fowler wanted Krystal to come home. Every year for the last five years. Krystal asked for money and never came home. But this year, Mrs. Fowler might have been Krystal's one phone call. The money she'd wired could have been for Krystal's bail.

Jay — whoever he was — had said Krystal was in trouble because of Mrs. Fowler. Because Celia Fowler had abandoned her and not cared for her? Or did it have to do with Krystal's recent arrest? For a distant relative, he knew a lot about Krystal, Mrs. Fowler, and Martha Mae.

And why hadn't Mrs. Fowler taken Krystal into her home if her mother had been a junkie?

That really bothered me. I didn't have a grandmother.

Daddy's mother had died when he was in college. Cancer. And Vicki's had been hit by a bus sometime when I was a toddler. Which always unsettled me, so I didn't like to think about it. Vicki never encouraged me to ask about her. I'd imagined my dead grandmothers as a cross between Mrs. Werther and Mrs. Butterworth.

Maybe because I spent a lot of my childhood forced to resist candy and carbs.

A pony-tailed waitress stood before me, coffee carafe in hand. "Warm you up?"

I wish. The last time I'd been this cold had been Sundance. I had been invited to a cast party and ended the night passed out in a snowbank.

"Thanks." I shoved the cup toward her. "I guess it's pretty quiet today because of the weather."

She nodded. "That and the bank robbery. Spooked everyone."

"Robbery?" I tipped my head back to get a good look at the server. "What happened?"

"Local bank. Everyone was cashing in their Christmas bonus today, too, since most are off work tomorrow and Christmas."

"Wow," I said. "Just like in the movies."

She gave me a look that told me she thought I was about as smart as my waffle. "Cop was taken hostage, too."

"Oh no," I said. "Is he or she okay?"

"He. They've still got him as far as I know. Been trying to listen in on the local radio, but they don't like to interrupt the Christmas music for news much. And they don't let us keep a TV in here."

"Why don't you use your phone?"

She gave me another look.

"I hope the police will save him," I said. "That's just terrible."

"Local boy, too." She shook her head.

"Sorry to hear about his girlfriend. Still, terrible."

She refilled my coffee.

"By the way," I asked. "Do you know Martha Mae Boyes? An older lady living in Halo?"

"We've got a lot of older ladies living in Halo." She gave me the side-eye. "Why?"

OMG, these Halo people were suspicious. "I'm working for her sister, Celia Fowler, who lives in Black Pine. Her sister called Martha Mae to say I was coming. I left Martha Mae a message myself, but she wasn't at home when I arrived. I waited, but now there's a man at her house. Jay. Jay said she's resting, but I don't know. It just seemed odd."

The waitress set her hands on her hips. "I don't know Miss Martha. But I doubt she'd get up to anything odd around here. Although it's been an odd day all around. This weather is terrible. And a robbery. Just don't seem like Christmas."

"Maybe it'll snow," I said helpfully.

"Good Lord, I hope not."

When the waitress had returned to lean against the counter and talk to the cook, I slid to the end of my booth and flipped open my phone.

"Where are you?" Nash's normal low rumble had pitched higher. "Did you slide off the road? I checked the reports and Atlanta's a mess. Do you need my help?"

"I'm in a Waffle Hut. I haven't left Halo."

He gusted a sigh. "Don't wait much longer. Get your coffee to go. Take it slow. I'm not sure if you should risk local highways. Stick to the interstate, but don't go through Atlanta if you can avoid it."

"You're worried about me." My toes curled inside my boots.

"Of course, I'm worried about you." He'd been pacing because his heavy tromp suddenly stopped. "There's weather."

I grinned at my phone. Why did I love that he was worried? Vicki would say it was chauvinist — women doing it for themselves, you know — but I thought it adorbs. Renata would probably have something to say about that, too. "Father absence syndrome." But I didn't care. Totally adorbs.

Also, I was totally off track. Still sitting in an overheated Waffle Hut in the middle of nowhere with a suspicious man in an elderly lady's house. I told myself to focus. "Here's the thing."

"What happened?"

"There's a man at Martha Mae's house. He said Martha Mae was resting and didn't want to talk. Kind of strange, right?"

"I don't know Martha Mae, so I can't say for sure."

"Just believe me, he was strange. And he said Mrs. Fowler was the reason Krystal was in trouble. Nash, Mrs. Fowler didn't take Krystal in."

"I'm not following." He paused. "Trouble now or trouble earlier?"

"I don't know. I'm worried."

"Let's get you home, then worry. I don't like this weather."

"Nobody does. I don't think I'm ready to leave just yet. I don't like what's going on here. Did you ever check into Mrs. Fowler? Did Krystal have an arraignment yet? Could she be out on bail?"

I waited a beat. "Nash?"

"I never vetted Celia Fowler," he spoke slowly. "And I only looked up the arrest. I didn't check to see if Krystal had made bail. Dammit." Nash swore again. "Miss Albright. Maizie. It's not our problem."

"Can you do some research? I'd really like to know what Jay meant by Mrs. Fowler causing Krystal trouble. Why wouldn't a grandmother take in her grandchild if she didn't have a father and the mother was a junkie? Why would a grandmother not help her granddaughter?" I checked my rising pitch and lowered my voice. "And what about Martha Mae? She knew I was coming. Why wouldn't she talk to me? Nash, I'm—"

"I know. You're worried." The deep voice steadied into a soothing murmur. "Listen, give me a minute. I'll see if I can find anything about Mrs. Fowler for you. You might need to camp out in Halo. Is there a motel?"

"I can't afford a motel."

"We'll expense it."

Wow. Nash didn't expense anything that couldn't be billed to a customer. I felt a flush heat the back of my neck. "But I think I should continue to watch Martha Mae's house."

"What are the roads like?"

I glanced out the window next to me, watching the wind pelt icy rain against Tiffany's Pontiac. "Not too bad. And it's cozy in Tiffany's car."

"Don't forget to fill it up. Sometimes gas stations in small towns close down for the holidays and bad weather."

"Right." File that under things I never thought about. "Good idea. And Nash?"

"Yes, Miss Albright?" His low drawl caressed my ears.

"If I'm late getting back, I'm sorry."

"Better to be safe than sorry, right?"

"Yes." The flush heated my cheeks now. "I meant late for that other thing you mentioned earlier. For when I returned…"

He cleared his throat. "We won't worry about that now."

Hells. "We won't? But—"

"Let me work on Mrs. Fowler and Krystal. I'll call you back."

"You will?"

"Always." He cleared his throat. "I mean, of course. You have a phone charger for that car?"

"Yes." I didn't want to hang up. His voice was making me forget how wet and cold and miserable I was about to be. "Are you in the office? Is Lamar with you?"

"I guess we're predictable."

I smiled. "I like predictable. My therapist Renata says it's because I didn't have a lot of stability…never mind. But I'm glad Lamar is with you."

"Why?"

The heat rushed from my cheeks to my chest and prickled my neck. I didn't want Nash to be alone during the holidays. But telling him felt too personal. Too intimate. For now, anyway. "Um, tell Lamar he should try a red velvet for the donut shop. It's very seasonal."

He took a beat to digest the comment. "All right. Anything else, Miss Albright?"

"There was a bank robbery in town."

"In Black Pine?" I heard him tromp and the creak of his noisy door. "Lamar. Bank robbery."

Nash must have been speaking in his office with the door shut. Odd. Normally, he lets Lamar hear everything.

"No, here in Halo. Surprising for a little town, don't you think? But the waitress said most people cash their Christmas bonuses today. I guess the robbers knew it. They took a local cop hostage."

"Were they arrested? Is the officer okay?"

"I don't know. The waitress didn't have an update, but last she heard, they still had the officer."

"Sounds like a standoff. It'll get ugly. The holidays are always rough for law enforcement and to combine this with the weather? Damn. I'll check the news. Atlanta might've picked up the story. Wherever that bank is, stay clear."

"I'm headed back to watch Martha Mae's house. Some other neighbors are home. I might talk to them and see if they know anything about the man in her house. He gave me bad vibes."

"Vibes." A door closed. He must have reentered his office. "It's good to trust your instincts when feeling someone out, but don't jump to any conclusions. And don't rush into a situation. Just keep watch."

"But—"

"We both have a job to do. I'm going to do mine and get back to you. And when I call, I expect to hear the same from you. No — What do you call it? — no improv. This man at Martha Mae's house, Jay, does he have a last name?"

"He wasn't forthcoming with Jay, let alone a surname. That's part of the bad vibes."

"All the more reason to leave him be. You have a bad habit of following instincts instead of procedure."

"But my instincts are usually right. I've got good instincts."

"They're also dangerous. If you have bad vibes, stay away from this man, Maizie. Your bad vibes make me crazy."

That almost sounded hot. But admitting that made me sound desperate, so forget it.

DANGEROUS VIBES ASIDE, I felt it couldn't hurt to speak to the other neighbors, particularly the home of the pregnant woman. She'd gone to Martha Mae's house and spoken to Jay. These small towns were tight. Surely, they'd give me some insight into Jay's relationship to Martha Mae. Or some background into Jay. He knew Krystal and Mrs. Fowler. But something wasn't right with him.

I tried the pregnant woman first. When I returned to Martha Mae's street — fishtailing over progressively slick roads — the truck was still gone, but the old Firebird remained. I took it as a good sign and pulled in behind the Firebird. The broken umbrella made a half-hearted fight against the rain then blew inside out. I slid-walked up the drive. Shivering, I rang the doorbell and hopped from foot to foot. Although in need of paint and repair, the porch was clean. A small, brightly colored table sat between two rocking chairs, also hand-painted with abstract designs and flowers.

But no wreath, no porch lights, no Santa Snoopy. I wondered what the other neighbors thought. The absence of decorations disturbed me. In this town of wooden nativities and inflatable polar bears, it seemed a flagrant disregard of holiday spirit.

The pregnant woman answered the door. She wore a tank top that barely covered her baby bump. It read, "One of Santa's ho's." Vicki would not approve. I wasn't going to judge. Maybe with the pregnancy, she had no time to put up a tree or decorations and chosen ironic holiday slogans in maternity wear instead.

"Who're you?" she said.

"I'm Maizie. I work for a private investigator in Black Pine. Mrs. Boyes's sister hired me to check on Martha Mae."

Proud of my ability to introduce myself and my mission more coherently, I continued. "Mrs. Fowler, the sister, is worried about Martha Mae." Which wasn't really a lie. "She didn't answer her door earlier today although she was expecting me. And there's a man there now —Jay — but Mrs. Fowler didn't expect him. I was watching the house and saw you spoke to Jay, too. Do you know him?"

"I'm Casey." Her brown eyes narrowed, and she flipped her long chestnut mane behind her shoulder. "Interestin'."

"Can I come in?" I blew on my mittens.

"You can, but I don't know if you want to. My sister's got the flu. This house is probably what gave it to her. It's barely warmer in here than out there. There're leaks, too. I've got her paint pot sitting on the kitchen floor, catching drips. She won't move, though. Cherry's stubborn like that."

"Okay?" Was that an invitation or not? "I'll take my chances on the flu. You look warm enough."

"I'm hotter than a brick oven. You could bake a pizza on me." She stepped aside to allow me through the door. "My husband's sort-of Russian. Close enough to Russian for around here. Anyway, he says Slavic pregnancies are always like this. It's real cold up there in Russia. I have no idea if that's true, but I've been sweating up a storm since the second trimester."

"Congratulations?" I glanced around the room. The paint-splattered wooden floors looked original as did the plaster walls. The room was mostly bare but for a vintage fainting couch, an easel, and an old roll-top desk. The Pasadena anti-quers would've had a field day. A series of portraits covered the walls. I recognized the pregnant woman in one. "Who did these?"

"My sister, Cherry. She's an artist."

"The one with the flu?"

Casey nodded, gripped her lower back, and eased on to the fainting couch. "What's it like to work for a private investigator? We don't have anything like that around here. Sometimes Cherry looks into criminal problems for friends, but she usually gets into trouble with the sheriff's office for that."

"It's wonderful." I clasped my mittens together, then wrung my hands. "Well, mostly it's kind of boring. Due diligence work. Security systems. Serving subpoenas. Maybe not any more boring than other jobs. I don't know. My previous career hasn't given me a lot of experience with other jobs. But right now, we're working on a missing granddaughter case. That's what I always dreamed of."

"You've always dreamed of a missing granddaughter?"

"Helping people find missing persons."

"I hope you don't get too many of those." She wrinkled her nose. "My uncle is sheriff. I've heard about crime my whole life. It's horrible. Especially what they're dealing with today."

I checked my excitement. "I heard about the bank robbery. Did they arrest the suspects yet?"

Casey shook her head and lowered her voice. "Far as I know, they're holed up in the bank with one of our deputies. He offered himself in exchange for the customers they held hostage."

"Oh my God."

"The deputy's my sister's man." She folded her arms over her bump. "Keep your voice down. She doesn't know."

"Oh no." My hand flew to cover my mouth.

"We don't want to tell her," she whispered. "She's already sick with a high fever. Seeing crazy stuff. Knowing Cherry, she'll crawl out of bed, drive to the bank, and get herself killed."

"That poor woman."

"The sheriff's waiting on a special team who works with hostage situations. FBI, too. They're coming over from Atlanta, but the weather has slowed everything down. They want to be real careful with this group. I guess they've had a lot of experience in armed robbery. Warrants out on all of 'em. They're stuck inside right now. Going on two hours." Casey bit her lip, and her eyes shone. "They shot Melanie when she triggered the alarm. She's a cashier. Part-time, too. Sumbitches. We'll get 'em, though.

Luke's got a good head. He's ex-Army. And we've got them surrounded."

I hoped the deputy would be okay. The robbers would be desperate to get away.

"We're worried, though," she continued. "They won't put Luke on the phone and have threatened to kill him if the sheriff doesn't provide an escape. Their getaway driver took off when the alarm went off, near as we can figure. That was the last I heard. Pearl's gone to the Tru-Buy, hoping to get more information. I don't think Uncle Will can wait for the Atlanta team to get here."

Tears pricked my eyes, and I pinched the skin between my thumb and finger. "I'm so sorry. I hate to be bothering you at a time like this."

"Y'all want something hot to drink? Cherry don't have much, but I can rustle you up something." Casey pushed herself into standing. "I don't know why I'm telling you this. I guess I'm just desperate to talk about it and I can't say a word to Cherry."

"Don't make anything. I just came from the Waffle Hut." I hesitated, hating to bring up the neighbors with the anxiety she must already feel. "About Martha Mae next door. Do you know her well? Or Jay?"

"The nephew? Cherry thought something was going on over there, too, but she's half-crazy with that fever. Jay's staying with Mrs. Boyes's for the holiday. She hurt her back."

"Oh. Nephew." Nash was right about me jumping to conclusions. Again. But then, why didn't Jay tell me he was a nephew? Didn't he say distantly related? "I guess you know Jay."

"Naw. Never seen him before. But I went over there to see what was going on. I'm going to make them a casserole soon as I get home."

"Do you know Krystal, Martha Mae's grand-niece? She's the missing granddaughter. I was supposed to talk to Mrs. Boyes's about that today."

"Never heard of her."

I moved toward the door. "I really appreciate your help. You'll probably see my car on the street. Until I know more, I'm going to watch Martha Mae's house. My partner's checking to see if Krystal's out."

"Out?"

"She was arrested three days ago. We don't know if she's in jail or out on bail."

Casey shivered and crossed her arms. "Too many criminals running around here for my liking."

"Don't worry. If I see anything suspicious, I'll call it in."

"Good luck getting anybody to help. They're all over at the bank."

#OLittleTownofHalo

THE OTHER NEIGHBOR, Josiah Sweeton, knew nothing about Krystal or Martha Mae's alleged-nephew, Jay. I say alleged because there was something fishy going on over there. Back in California, I knew of a few "nephews" who helped their "aunts" or "uncles" for whatever reason. You learn not to ask a lot of questions in those cases. You just don't want to know. But this wasn't Beverly Hills. This was Halo, Georgia. And in Beverly Hills, the "nephews" were younger and better looking than Jay.

Possibly Martha Mae was into something weird. Not judging. But Jay knew Krystal. Krystal was not a nun (as far as I knew). And it sounded like nobody else around here knew Jay or Krystal, but they knew Martha Mae. If Martha Mae was into something weird, I felt certain the neighbors would've hinted at it. Or at least made the quote sign when stating, "nephew."

Therefore, I was worried about Mrs. Boyes. And she didn't answer her phone. If her back was out, maybe she couldn't pick up. But wouldn't Jay check to find out who kept leaving voicemails?

I moved Tiffany's car in a less obtrusive spot down the street where I could keep an eye on Martha Mae's house. Using a pile of napkins that I had taken from the Waffle Hut, I dried myself as best I could, cranked the heater, and watched the house. Checked my phone six times to make sure it was still charged. Then checked again to see if I had bars. And a dial tone. Played Christmas music. Imagined warm thoughts.

Maybe me and Nash under the mistletoe. But I won't go there. Tired of waiting, I called Nash.

"Any news?" I said.

"I can't find anything about the robbery," said Nash. "Maybe the local law enforcement is keeping the story under wraps."

"Maybe they captured the criminals, and the deputy is home. Everyone is worried. What about Mrs. Fowler and Krystal?"

"You were right. Krystal was arrested on December twentieth. Petty theft charge. Didn't have to make bail. At her preliminary hearing, the charges were dropped. Guess she hadn't changed her tune. She didn't have much of a record, surprisingly."

I chewed my lip. "So, she's out."

"Mrs. Fowler doesn't have a record. But her husband did. Hinky."

Hinky was Nash-speak for suspicious.

"I also checked on Martha Mae," he said. "She's clean. Married someone from down around Halo. He worked at a sweet tea factory. She's a widow. No kids."

"So sad. And now she has to spend Christmas with an alleged nephew. Poor Martha Mae."

He gave me a minute to get over the state of Martha Mae's life. "I don't know where this Jay fellow comes in. If he's a nephew, he's got to be from the husband's side. We know he's not on Martha Mae's side since it's just the two sisters."

"Right? And he's not a 'nephew.'" I made quote signs and

realized it didn't work on a phone. At least a phone that didn't have video chat.

"I thought you said he's a nephew," said Nash.

"Never mind. But if Jay was a relative on Martha Mae's husband's side, why would he know Krystal?"

"It's hinky." He paused. "You should come home. But now you can't."

"I can't?"

"The storm's come to the mountains. And the rain you just had is snow here. It's icing over something terrible."

"Yay, white Christmas for Remi." I smiled then frowned. "Oh no, I've got to get home tomorrow. Remi is expecting me."

"Tomorrow. Get a motel room. They'll scoop tomorrow. At least in the mountains."

"It's still early."

"I don't like you being all the way over there." He cleared his throat. "I don't have a good feeling about Mrs. Fowler. "

"Mrs. Fowler didn't help Krystal when Krystal needed her."

"That and her husband used to rob banks."

"Used to?"

"He's dead. Died in prison."

"Oh." I felt some sympathy for Mrs. Fowler even though I still felt she should have been a better grandmother. She had her own baggage. But still. "At least we know he's not involved with this bank robbery because that'd be super hinky, right?"

No sound.

"Nash?"

"Right." He took a breath. "Find a motel room. I'm going to do more research."

HALO DIDN'T HAVE MOTELS. Or inns. Or stables. I didn't want to travel to another town. I was also concerned with bank robbery traffic. There wasn't traffic in Halo, but with my luck, I'd get stuck. The neighbors didn't seem to care that I parked in front of their house. Or notice. The Hallmark Channel had given me the impression that small towns were full of nosy neighbors. Nosy but caring. Why weren't Martha Mae's neighbors paying any attention to me?

Not that I was complaining. I didn't want to get run out of town. I wanted to know that sweet Martha Mae — who I'm sure would've made a wonderful grandmother if given a chance — was really flat on her back.

Not that I wished her a back injury. It'd just make me feel better.

All was quiet at Martha Mae's. The lights were still on in the living room. The tree still blinked. But there was no other movement. What was Jay doing? Taking a nap? The other houses showed signs of life. TVs lit front rooms. Lights flicked on and off. Shadows crossed before windows. But at Martha Mae's, nothing. The temperature continued to drop, but the rain had stopped. I took it as a sign to get out and explore Martha Mae's again. Also, my legs were cramping because I had curled them underneath myself to stay warm.

Outside the car, I unbent and did a quick yoga sun salutation. No sun appeared. Just moist, frigid air. Not a fav. But it cleared my lungs and my mind. I needed to get inside the house. To see if Martha Mae was okay, I told myself. That was legit. Right? Without a car, it was difficult to tell if Jay was even home. Martha Mae's Buick still sat in the drive, but judging by the coat of ice, it hadn't moved since lunchtime.

I scooted across the street and down the sidewalk toward Martha Mae's. The sidewalk was slick. The grass crunchy. On Martha Mae's porch, I peeked into the living room window. No movement except for the bubbling lights of the tree. I knocked on the door. Quietly. Tried the knob. Locked.

No one home. Except for Martha Mae, if her back was really out. I knew where Martha Mae kept her key. I hesitated on the porch. The wind rattled the frosted Christmas lights. I was totally overstepping my bounds. But sometimes a girl's just got to break-and-enter. To help the elderly. At Christmas.

A truck roared up the street and turned at the drive into the pregnant woman's sister's house. I backed against the front door. Corrected my flattened stance to a casual lean. Waited for a minute. Sauntered to the edge of the porch to examine the Christmas lights. Heard a door slam next door. Walked back to the door and waited another minute. And scurried to the porch steps to steal — I mean borrow — the key.

9 CHERRY TUCKER

"THERE'S something weird going on in Mrs. Boyes's house," I told Pearl. She'd returned with weapons for battling the flu. Cans of Lysol, bottles of Tylenol, and applesauce.

"It's all in your head," said Pearl. "You're burning up with fever and we've got to get that temperature down. If you don't cool off, I'm tossing you in a tub of ice."

My skin broke into goose pimples. "You try to throw me in a tub of ice and I'll fight you." I pulled out a fist and returned it under the blanket. My teeth chattered. "Plus, I've got the Remington under my bed. Be warned."

She waved away my threat. "You can barely sit up. You don't have the strength to pull out a shotgun, let alone the cajones. You want to exchange threats, I'll bring Snickerdoodle over and park her in your kitchen."

Snickerdoodle was Pearl's evil goat, the terror of Grandpa Ed's barnyard. Her offspring were devil's spawn. They hated me and my truck. Snickerdoodle scared the bejeesus out of me, but I'd never admit that to Pearl.

I fell back against my pillow. "I probably have the goat flu as it is. This feels worse than human flu."

"Goats are too smart to get the flu. That's for chickens and pigs." Pearl shoved a green Gatorade toward me. "You need fluids."

My stomach cramped. I pointed a trembling finger at my window, hoping to get Pearl off the subject of fluids. "A woman was in Mrs. Boyes's house while you were out. An out-of-towner. The nephew invited her in and she looked around like she was taking inventory."

"Martha Mae's house? Of all the nerve." Pearl dropped the Gatorade on my bed and stomped to the window. "Who is this woman prying into poor Martha Mae's house?"

"I don't know," I said. "She looked like a movie star. Except wet."

"Everyone's wet today." Pearl glanced back at me. "Are you sure you saw this woman? Not another hallucination?"

"Pretty sure." I struggled to push myself up and collapsed against my pillow. "The nephew let her in. She looked around and then left."

Pearl turned back to the window. "What's a movie star doing in Martha Mae's house? What did she say?"

"I'll go over and ask Mrs. Boyes. As soon as I'm over this flu."

"Don't get sassy with me." Pearl tapped her chin. "I wonder what Gertie Sweetley will say about this. She's Martha Mae's best friend, but a terrible gossip. We do the bingo together."

"Maybe you should ask her yourself."

"Is this nephew staying for Christmas?"

"I hope so." I closed my eyes. "Casey said Mrs. Boyes's back is out."

"Casey said?" Pearl whipped around. "What does Casey know about this?"

"I asked her to go check on Mrs. Boyes. Because of... you know, what I thought I saw."

"Casey should not be walking around in this weather. She's just about nekkid."

"Casey's used to being 'just about nekkid,'" I mumbled. "It's her signature style."

"She is carrying your niece or nephew. Casey could slip and fall. It is getting icier than a Tastee Freeze out there."

"Sorry," I muttered. "You're right."

"I'll go over there myself. If Martha Mae's back is out, she's going to need help. That nephew probably don't know up from down."

"I don't think that's a good id—"

Pearl was gone before I could get the words out.

#RunRunRudolph

I RETRIEVED the key from under the poinsettia. Shoved it quietly (as was possible) into the lock. Cracked the door and whispered a "Hello? Mrs. Boyes? Martha Mae?"

Nada. Maybe due to the extra quiet nature of my call. But still. I took it as an all-clear sign.

Tiptoeing, I sped through the living room and peeked into the dining room. Glanced into the empty kitchen. Smelled like gingerbread. More evidence that if only Martha Mae'd had children, she'd get the grandmother-of-the-year award. Peeked into the hall. A double row of closed doors. I took a deep breath.

Here's where it got tricky. I had bad luck with closed doors.

I crept down the hall and placed an ear near the edge of the first door. No sound. Sniffed. Caught a hint of lavender. Rotated the knob slowly.

Bathroom. Papered in pink and purple flowers. And decorated for Christmas. Martha Mae had a Grinch toilet seat cover. Adorbs.

I left the bathroom open and sidled to the next door. This was the room where earlier I had seen lights. A low murmur, then music blared through the closed door. The volume lowered. Someone watched TV. The commercials were always louder than the shows. Maybe Martha Mae? Should I pop in? I didn't want to scare the woman. I was just looking for evidence that Jay was legit. And I needed to warn Martha Mae about Krystal.

Hello, Maizie. You're also trespassing. And on probation. Trespassing is not cool with probation officers.

Worrying my lip, I moved toward the other side of the hall. Listened. Couldn't hear anything. A bell ping-ponged. I froze before the closed door.

Doorbell. Shizzles. And there it went again.

I sensed a stirring behind the door with the TV. I yanked open the door before me and darted inside. Bedroom. I waited for my eyes to adjust to the lack of light. No one called out or moved. That was good. My heart slowed from sprint to marathon beat. I rubbed a mitten on the back of my neck.

One silver lining to trespassing: the adrenaline kick sure warmed a body up.

The bell rang again. Knocking commenced.

I placed my eye against the crack in the door. Saw nothing but the closed door opposite.

"Yoo-hoo, Martha Mae?" A woman called from the front of the house. Her voice grew louder with each word. "Y'all home? It's Pearl. I'm visiting Cherry next door."

Craptastic. I had left the door unlocked. Who was Pearl?

"I understand your nephew is there. Maybe he's gone now. I just wanted to check on you. I know you can't get up. I'll come to you."

The door across the hall opened. I squinted through the crack, but my view was blocked. Someone hurried down the hall. An exchange began between Pearl and Jay.

Holy shiz. A chill crawled up my neck. Jay was home. He could've caught me roaming the hall. My heart hammered against my ribs. Back to sprint. And I was now perspiring. I needed to get out of this house.

What in the hellsbah was I thinking? House-crashing some poor grandma and her nephew?

But with Pearl occupying Jay, wouldn't this be a good opportunity to check on Martha Mae? Just in case my intuition had been correct? Jay sounded intent on keeping Pearl from seeing her friend. Wasn't that weird?

So hard to judge weird in a town I didn't know. But I couldn't leave Martha Mae without checking on her first.

I slipped out the bedroom door. Poked my head into the room opposite that Jay had just exited. Looked like a master bedroom. A small TV on top of a dresser provided the only light in the cavernous room. The volume was almost muted. Curtains had been pulled across the shaded windows. I squinted into the dark. The bed faced the front of the house, but the room behind it jutted out from the hall, blocking my view of the bed other than the foot. There was a shape on the bed, but I couldn't make out if it were a person or bedding.

"Martha Mae?" I whispered. "Are you in there? Are you okay?"

The voices in the front room climbed. Pearl was arguing with Jay about hot compresses and his apparent ignorance on the subject.

I took a step into the room, inching along the wall. "Martha Mae? Your sister sent me. I left you a bunch of messages. Has your niece Krystal been here? You need to know she might show at your house and she's been in some trouble."

Why didn't Martha Mae say anything? Was she hiding?

Of course. She probably thought I was a crazy person.

"I'll just take a second." Pearl's voice had grown louder. "And let me peek into your kitchen pantry to see what y'all need. I'm sure you haven't thought of everything, son. Are you prepared to ride out this storm?"

Holy Shizzolis. Jay and Pearl were going to find me in

Martha Mae's bedroom. I froze against the bedroom wall. Inched back toward the door.

"What's that?" said Pearl. "What're you doing?"

Where was Pearl? In the kitchen? How was I going to explain myself? I peeked into the hall. Empty. I darted back to the other bedroom. Closed the door and leaned against it, panting.

OMG, I ran like three steps, and I'm panting?

Focus Maizie. When they go into the bedroom to visit Martha Mae, get the hells out of the house. Martha Mae didn't want your help.

Why did I still have the feeling there was something odd going on? Was Martha Mae even in there?

A loud bang shook the walls. My heart leaped from my chest to my throat. Something heavy thudded against the floor.

What in the holy shiz was that?

I clapped my hand over my mouth to keep from crying out. It sounded like a piece of furniture had been knocked over. More than one. A dining set? A refrigerator? I placed my ear to the door. What was that sound? Were they moving furniture?

Pearl wasn't talking. She had talked the entire time she was here. Why wasn't she talking?

Okay. Loud Pearl was now totally silent. Martha Mae was also quiet. And weird Jay was somewhere in the house.

OMG.

"Do something, dumbass," said my snarky, inner Julia Pinkerton.

I turned on the overhead light and glanced around the bedroom. A host of Santa dolls dressed in long underwear decorated the flat surfaces. Quilts covered the walls. A box of gift bags lay on the bed. Martha Mae wrapped presents in here. Scissors. She'll have scissors. I pawed through the tissue paper and ribbons. Found a box of candy canes. Grabbed a stick.

What was I going to do with a candy cane? Focus, Maizie.

I shoved the candy cane into my pocket and rummaged through the box. No scissors.

Seriously Martha Mae? You never used wrapping paper?

Sometimes it's nice to have a box wrapped in ribbon and not just a gift shoved in a bag with a piece of tissue paper.

Maizie, stop judging this poor grandma. She could have arthritis, for God's sake. You're just panicking.

The bedside table held a Santa in a rocking chair, hand on his stomach, and eyes closed. Long Winter's Nap Santa. No scissors. I opened the dresser drawers. Quilts. Folded material. Material cut into squares. Another drawer of material. This time in rolls.

Martha Mae sewed stuff. She must have scissors. Something sharp.

Another drawer revealed rows and rows of thread. One roll of masking tape. The narrow drawers on top held tiny boxes. Straight pins. Tiny gold safety pins. Needles. In various sizes but all small and slender.

OMG, Martha Mae. Unless I had a blow dart these sharp objects were useless.

I broke off the hook of the candy cane, tore off a bunch of masking tape, and wrapped the tape around the stick. Stared at the masked stick in my hand.

In my head, Julia Pinkerton laughed. "Seriously? What are you going to do with that?"

I shoved the candy cane back in my pocket.

Taking a deep yoga breath, I forced myself to calm. I was jumping to conclusions, just like Nash had warned. Of course, he'd also told me to do nothing but watch. Which is why I had left the phone in the car.

Craptastic. My phone was in the car.

I returned to the door. Listened. The furniture-moving sounds had stopped. All quiet. Placed my hand on the door-knob. Said a quick prayer. Rotated the knob. Heard a door slam on the other side of the house.

Took my hand off the knob, turned off the light, and set my back against the door. Blood hammered inside my ears. Sweat pooled beneath my beanie.

My eyes darted around Martha Mae's craft storage/guest

room. In the dark, I felt six pairs of Santa eyes watching me. Except for Long Winter's Nap Santa whose eyes were closed.

Faint light rimmed the window.

I ran to the window, grabbed the string for the shade, and ran the louvers to the top. The window looked newish. Easy to open. There was a screen, but that could be removed. I unlatched the window, pushed it as high as it would go. Cold air whistled past me. I squeezed the screen's spring latches. Gave it a push, up and out. The screen struck something and fell to the ground outside. I stuck my head through the opening. Wind rushed past me, chafing my cheeks. There was a bush below the window. Covered in net lights.

At least the neighbors behind Martha Mae's house couldn't witness my escape. I could just make out their lights past a stand of trees in Martha Mae's backyard. If this were the side of the house, the artist's home next door was spitting distance. Silver lining.

The window was waist high. I threw a leg up. With an over loud thud, my boot heel hit the sill and scuffed the white paint. Wind blew into the room, rattling the paper bags and ruffling the tissue paper. I turned and hoisted my seat onto the ledge, grabbed the window frame, and inched my butt through the window. When my back hit air, I angled my sit and bent my left leg. I was not going through this window backward. No trust fall into a bush. I didn't know the bush, let alone want to get tangled in a bunch of netted lights. Martha Mae had put a lot of work into Christmas-fying her house and I didn't want to screw it up.

Poor Martha Mae.

With one butt cheek in the open air and the other wedged against the window frame, I eased my left foot onto the ledge and wiggled my bent leg toward the opening. Bent the right leg and got both feet onto the ledge. My knees threatened to hit my chin. I scooted to turn toward the open air.

The bedroom door creaked.

I pushed off the window and fell into the bush. Face first.

Tangled with the lights and rolled toward the house, pulling them with me. Wrapped in net lighting, I squeezed between the bush and the house. The tiny lights blinded me. And totally lit my whole body. I might as well have a blinking neon arrow pointed to my hiding spot. I yanked on the cord and pulled a net off the next bush. Scrabbled with the net to push the lights off my face. Pulled off my mitten, grabbed a tiny bulb, and twisted. The bulb popped out.

The entire back of the house went dark.

I'll fix that later, Martha Mae.

I dropped the bulb. And lost my mitten.

Never mind, Martha Mae.

Above me, something hit the window. I looked up. Two dark hands silhouetted against the white frame. Rolled in net lighting, I flattened against the house and held my breath. A shape appeared in the window. Jay leaned out, craning his neck right and left. He retreated. The window shut with a slam.

On the frigid, soggy ground, I tried not to think about the icy mud oozing up my sides and coating my coat, jeans, and boots. I waited what seemed like hours — realistically, maybe thirty seconds — then wriggled from behind the bush. Fought the net lighting. I slithered out. Kicked the lighting behind the bush.

Then ran toward the house next door.

11 CHERRY TUCKER

FROM MY BED, I studied the scene through the window. The movie star had returned. Uninvited. Skulking. At least that's what it looked like. No one let her in. She snuck in. Skittered through Martha Mae's living room and disappeared.

Dammit. What was she up to? Should I call the police? That's a B and E if there ever was one. Was she going to rob Martha Mae?

I glanced at the phone on my bedside table. Call 9-1-1? Maybe get Casey to do it this time. They were going to think I was like that shepherd boy who pranked villagers with wolf stories. Even though I wasn't goofing off. Something funny was going on at Mrs. Boyes's house.

"Case." My voice warbled, frail and thin. Lord, I hated this weakness.

Casey appeared in the bedroom door. She held a string of lights in her hand.

"Found lights. And a little tree. You'd shoved Great Gam's boxes in the back of the guest room closet," she said. "Where do you want them?"

I ignored her and focused on the window opposite. "Something is going on at that house again."

"I'm going to put some lights up in here. It'll make you feel better. You seem to like looking at Mrs. Boyes's tree." She sauntered into the room. "Just don't cough on me or anything."

"Don't you want to know what's going on over there?"

"Not really." She gazed about my bedroom. "I don't know why you don't decorate. It's punishing you, not her."

I snuggled deeper into my quilt and rested my chin on my knees. "Most decorations are tacky. Or insipid. Not my cup of tea."

"I thought you were an artist. You could make your own holiday decorations." Casey stood before the window. "Paint a Christmas scene or something."

I waved a hand. "You're blocking my view."

"I don't think she chose to leave us at Christmas on purpose. Momma wasn't that mean. Maybe she thought it'd take our minds off her going."

"I'm sick." I slithered beneath the quilt. "Hang the lights or not, but I'm not up for psychoanalysis if you don't mind."

Casey held up the lights, eyeballing spots on the wall. "Just trying to help. I try to think about all the Christmases Grandma Jo made special for us. She put a lot of effort into Christmas."

"I know." Propping my head on my hand, I tried to see above the window sill. Gave up. Sat up and squinted at the window. "That makes it even harder."

"I thought you hated Christmas because of Momma. It's because of Grandma Jo dying so young?"

I sighed. "Both, I guess. I'm just tired of being lonely."

"You don't have to be lonely. Luke—" Casey cut herself off. "Maybe we shouldn't decorate your house just now."

I cranked up an eyebrow. "Why? Don't tell me it's because you're agreeing with me because I know you better than that."

"They remind you of bad times, and you're feeling bad anyway. Maybe I shouldn't push it." Casey wound the lights around her arm. "Christmas should make you happy."

"But you're right. I should think of the good Christmases we had with Grandma Jo and Grandpa Ed. Not what we missed out on." I studied the blinking tree through my window. "Everything looks warm and friendly over at Mrs. Boyes's house. But I think something cold and sinister is going on over there. Decorating can't cover that up."

Casey glanced over her shoulder, eyeing the scene on the other side of the window. "I don't see anything. And the nephew is helping Mrs. Boyes out. That's good Christmas spirit." She turned back to study me. "I think I need to close these curtains."

"No," I cried. "I need to know what's going on."

"Don't excite yourself." She bit her lip. "I'll leave them open for now. Lord knows you'll climb out of bed to open them as soon as my back is turned. I don't want you getting up. Let me hang these lights, then you rest."

I nodded, my attention fixed on the window. The rain had stopped, but the windows were icing.

Casey plugged the lights into my bedside socket. "What do you think is going on at Mrs. Boyes's now?"

"An out-of-towner's over there. Some fancy woman. She just broke into Mrs. Boyes's house."

"A what?" Casey dropped the lights and turned to face the window. "Wait. A redhead? She came over to ask about Mrs. Boyes. Her name's Maizie, and she's a private investigator. Mrs. Boyes's sister hired the investigator to find her granddaughter. The sister sent Maizie down from Black Pine to warn Mrs. Boyes about the granddaughter."

"Private investigators don't break into people's houses, Casey. She must be lying."

Casey massaged her lower back. "I don't know. I talked to her a bit. Seemed nice enough. Maybe she's in the house to check on Mrs. Boyes. The granddaughter's out on bail. Maizie seemed genuinely worried about Mrs. Boyes."

"I don't like it." I scooted to the edge of the bed and dipped a toe into the cold air. Shivering, I slipped my other foot off the bed. Pulling my blankets around my shoulders, I sat on the edge of the bed, gathering strength. "I'm going over there."

Casey whipped around. "Get back in bed."

"Don't try to stop me. There's funny business going on at Mrs. Boyes's house. I haven't seen Mrs. Boyes since Santa killed the reindeer. Now there's a movie star snooping around." Dizzy, I dipped my head and panted. "Just give me a minute."

"I'm stopping you." Casey strode to the bed, placed a hand on my forehead, and flicked it off. "You're burning up. Did you take that medicine Pearl got you?"

"I don't remember." I sniffled. "Where's Pearl?"

"Lord, if you're crying over Pearl, you're seriously ill." Casey pulled the covers off my shoulders and shoved me back onto the bed. "Now climb in. Take your medicine. Drink your Gatorade. And stop being such a pain in the ass. You've never done what you're told when sick. Not even as a child. Just lie down."

"Casey," I said. "I'm serious. Where's Pearl?"

"She went out a minute ago." Half-turned, Casey's anger faded. Her eyes narrowed, and she shot back to the window. "Dammit, Pearl's there now. I told her I already went over. What is she doing?"

I lay on my back, panting. "Pearl will find the movie star."

"She's arguing with that nephew." Casey laughed. "This is pretty funny to watch. I wonder what's she saying? Probably telling him, 'Son, you need to soak your aunt in goat's milk.' Or some such goat nonsense."

I closed my eyes. "Prob'ly."

"Now she's marching toward the kitchen. Fixin' to cook. Or inventory their supplies." Casey sucked in her breath. "The nephew's following. He looks madder than spit."

Dreams interfered with Casey's play-by-play. I saw Santa, his eyes narrowed, lips pulled back in a snarl. Yanking the Christmas lights tight in his hands. Flinging it around the reindeer's throat. I drifted.

"Wake up," said Casey. "Cherry, wake up."

My eyes flew open. "What?"

Casey sat on the edge of my bed. "The nephew and Pearl were gone for a minute, then he came back into the living room alone. I don't know what Pearl is doing. The nephew saw me, watching. And now he's moving the tree in front of the window."

"Serves us right, I guess." I couldn't pull my thoughts together. Colored light shone on Casey. I looked up and saw the string of lights had been flung over Snug. The cord dangled down the wall. "Wait a minute. Mrs. Boyes wouldn't want anybody moving her tree. She's very particular about decorating. She always has the tree in that corner."

"Never mind that." Casey's voice shook. She wrapped her arms around her belly. "Cherry, he saw me watching the house. The nephew. He pointed at me. Then drew his finger across his throat."

#WeNeedALittleChristmas #LikeRightNow

I WAS FAIRLY sure Jay hadn't seen me. Soon after I escaped Martha Mae's backyard, I heard a door slam. Scooting from my hiding spot behind a sawhorse in the next door carport, I slid-crept between the parked vehicles and watched Martha Mae's house. A minute later, Jay tramped off the porch and strode around the side of the house. He disappeared from view. Looking for whoever broke into the house.

Couldn't really blame him. Because it was a break-in. By me.

Keeping to the far side of the artist's driveway, I used the cover of the old yellow pickup, the Firebird, then the big truck to keep myself hidden. Ran across the road and down the street. Slid and almost fell six times. Ducked into Tiffany's car. With trembling fingers, I shoved the keys in the ignition. And stopped before turning on the engine.

Pearl. I bet she's the woman with the big truck. Casey, the pregnant woman, had mentioned her.

What had happened to Pearl?

I popped up my head to peer out the frosted windows. Martha Mae's living rooms lights were still on. I couldn't see Jay. In the sick artist's house, someone stood before the living room window. Hands around her eyes, looking out into the dark.

Ducking beneath the driver's side window, I glanced at my phone, wanting to call Nash.

And tell him you did exactly what he didn't want you to do? The man was already freaking out about the weather. Knowing Nash and his massive protection instincts, he'd drive hell-bent for Halo. The weather in the mountains would be much worse. I'd be risking his life.

Call the police? And tell them I — while on probation — illegally entered a woman's house and discovered…nothing useful for the police. They were busy with a serious bank robbery.

Maybe Pearl had stopped talking because she had gone back to the artist's house.

I blew on my mitten-less hand. The sweat I had accumulated running —Twenty yards? I so need to get back to the gym— now felt like a film of ice on my skin. But with Jay skulking about, I didn't want to draw attention to my car by turning it on.

I needed more information. First, see if Pearl is home.

Cracking the door, I slid out and kept low. Squat-walked on the sidewalk behind the car and peered around the side. The woman in the window was gone. I didn't see Jay.

"Coast is clear," I told myself. "Now just look normal. In case anyone is watching."

"Like it matters now," said my inner Julia Pinkerton.

Teenagers. Always the critic.

Straightening, I strolled around my car, then hurried across the street, sliding and slipping. With my arms windmilling, I reached their drive. Decided on the better traction of walking uphill in the crispy grass. I grabbed the railing on the front steps and hauled myself on to the porch. Rang the bell, then knocked.

Pregnant Casey peered out the window. I waved. She opened the door and dragged me inside.

"What in the hell happened to you?" she said. "You look like you fell in a goat pen. Why did you break into Mrs. Boyes's house? I trusted you. My sister wants to report you to the sheriff."

I raised my mittened hand. "Oh my God, please don't. I'm on probation. I'll probably get sent back to Beverly Hills to face Judge Ellis again."

Casey's penciled eyebrows hit her hairline. "I'm calling Uncle Will."

"It's totally cool. I used Martha Mae's key." I left off the part where Martha Mae hadn't given me the key. "I needed to check on Martha Mae. But I don't even know if she's in the house."

"The nephew said—"

"I know. But did you see her? Because I went into the bedroom — not all the way in, just the doorway, didn't want to scare poor Martha Mae — and called for her. I explained who I was and about Krystal. If anyone was in there — they've got the shades drawn, TV muted, lights off — they didn't respond. Does that sound like Martha Mae Boyes?"

Casey stuck a hand on her hip and sucked on her lip, considering. "It don't sound like Mrs. Boyes, I admit. She's like Pearl. Kind of loud. But in a friendly sort of way. Even to strangers. If you were already in her room, she'd say, 'Well, now that you're here, you might as well come on in. Let me tell you about my ruptured disc.'"

"See what I mean?" I clasped my hands together, then wiped my wet, bare hand on my dirty jeans.

"Maybe she took pain meds, and she's sleeping."

"But even sleeping people make some noise." I steepled my hands together and gave her my *American Girl Magazine* (circa 2000) smile. "I'm really trying to help Martha Mae. I have a bad feeling about her sister, her great-niece, and her nephew. Martha Mae's the only one in the family that doesn't set off my alarm bells. She really should've been a grandma."

"Huh," said Casey.

My smile stretched, froze, and dropped. "Niece and nephew. Distantly related nephew. Hang on. Sorry." Turning my back to Casey, I pulled out my phone. "Nash."

"Are you in a motel?"

My heart fluttered. I wished. That wasn't all I wished. Focus, Maizie.

"No. I'm in a house. Next door to Martha Mae. Everything's cool." I turned and smiled to Casey. "It's my boss, Wyatt Nash. He owns Nash Security Solutions in Black Pine."

"Who are you talking to?" said Nash.

"Martha Mae's neighbor, Casey."

"I don't live here," said Casey. "My sister, Cherry, does."

"The neighbor's sister."

"What's going on?" said Nash.

"Krystal's dad. You said he was in prison? Is he still in prison?"

"Dammit."

"So you'll get back to me on that?"

I snapped the phone shut and turned back to Casey. "I might have a lead on who Jay is."

She shuddered, then wrapped her hands around her belly. "The nephew moved the tree. He knows Cherry's been watching the house. And he saw me. Kind of threatened me."

"I thought I heard furniture moving." I paused. "But the living room is carpeted."

"Pearl went over there." Casey ran her hands up and down her arms. "And she's not back."

"Hells. I heard her talking to Jay, but I took off before I could help." I stared at my muddy boots. "I should've gone back in. Somehow."

"I think I should call Uncle Will. But the bank robbery—" Casey bit her lip and hugged her shoulders.

"Still a standoff?"

She shook her head. "Sheriff had to let them go. The FBI team didn't make it in time. The robbery gang threatened to kill Luke. Uncle Will negotiated a van for them. They dragged Luke out. Bound, gagged, and blindfolded. They all had guns aimed at him. Makes me sick. If they kill him, I don't know what Cherry will do. Why did this have to happen on Christmas?" She choked back a sob.

"What happened? Did they get away?"

Casey jerked a nod. "Uncle Will had our deputies and Line Creek police in unmarked vehicles waiting to follow them. They lost them for a minute. Then found the van headed toward the Winn Dixie on Highway Nineteen."

She took a deep breath. "But the robbers must've had different vehicles waiting. When the police followed them round to the back, the van had parked so law enforcement couldn't get around a big delivery truck. The robbers had gone inside the store, through the back, and out the front. The Winn Dixie was full of shoppers. Folks still stocking up for Christmas, worried about being totally iced over. The robbers split up and slipped out the front with the other shoppers."

"No one saw them?"

"At the bank, they were all dressed like Santa. They left the suits in the van."

"And the deputy held hostage?"

"Luke wasn't left in the van. Don't know where he is. They're studying the Winn Dixie's security tapes and interviewing the employees. But they think there might have been another car that met them before getting to the Winn Dixie." Casey shook her head, her eyes filled with tears. "I should call Uncle Will. But I don't know how serious this is next door. He's got his hands full with the search."

I hugged her. She felt warm and smelled like baby lotion. I could've used a longer hug. "You should go home. Take your sister with you. If it's serious—"

"Cherry shouldn't be out. Her fever is real high. I can't leave her. Nik is working tonight, or he'd come over. He wouldn't want me to drive the Firebird in this anyway. It's rear wheel drive."

"I'll stay with Cherry." I strode to the window and peered out.

"I'm not leaving my sister," said Casey. "No offense, but she doesn't trust you. And with that fever, I don't trust her."

"What would she do?"

"She finds you in her house, she'd probably shoot you. Cherry keeps a shotgun under her bed."

I LEFT Casey to check on Cherry — and hopefully to advise her sister not to shoot me. I'd met some crazy artists, but none with shotguns — and took a page from Nash's book. I paced before the window, thinking. If Jay was Krystal's father, why would he show up at Martha Mae's? Because he knew Krystal would show? If so, that meant I really couldn't leave. Was Krystal already there? What had happened to Martha Mae? And Pearl?

My phone rang. "What did you learn?"

"Merry Christmas to you, too, dear." My mother's honey-cloaked-in-steel drawl sounded tinny. "It's morning here. The jet lag is terrible. There's no Starbucks."

"Vicki, you're in Fiji. Drink the local coffee." I paused. "I mean, Merry Christmas. I really want to talk to you? But it's not a good time?"

"You're doing that uptalk thing again. Darling, you know it makes you sound stupid. Now, I have a list of things I need you to send me. Find a pen."

"Vicki. I'm on a case. A grandmother is missing. Maybe two. And a granddaughter. I can't talk."

"First, decent coffee. Second, Neiman's had a Kate Spade bikini that I almost ordered. I changed my mind. They have the audacity to say, they don't ship to Fiji. Unbelievable. So, I need you to express it to yourself and then express it to me. We're only here a week, so you'd better get on it."

"You're not hearing me." I pulled in a deep Ujjayi breath, held it five beats, and let it out. Renata said it would help to clear my mind and focus on the message, not the mother. "I'm waiting for another call. And I have to prepare myself for breaking and entering. Again."

"Is that a play? Are you auditioning?" Vicki paused. "Don't start back with stage work. Unless it's a charity gig. Are they paying? I'll negotiate—"

"It's not a play. It's a form of trespassing. And I have to go. Merry Christmas." I hung up on my manager. I mean, mother.

I'd not done that before. First time for everything.

OMG, Vicki was going to kill me. Thank God, she was in Fiji.

Casey walked in as I stared at the phone in my mittened palm. "What're you doing?"

"Calling my boss again." I quickly thumb dialed and cradled the phone against my ear. "Nash. What's Krystal's dad's name?"

"Jim Wiley."

"And he was in jail for?"

"Armed robbery. Got out three months ago."

Shizzles. "Krystal might be next door. I'm pretty sure Jim is Jay."

"Call the police."

"The police are a little busy with the bank robbery. The suspects escaped. And it's not illegal for Jay and Krystal to be next door. As far as we know. Although I'm not sure where Martha Mae went. Or Pearl."

"Dammit. Who's Pearl?"

"Actually, I'm not sure." I looked at Casey. "Who's Pearl?"

"Grandpa Ed's woman. She raises goats, too. That's the attraction, we figure."

"Pearl's a neighbor," I simplified.

"You're not going over there."

"Don't worry."

"Miss Albright, call the police. They can handle both emergencies. They're equipped."

"I don't think they have enough evidence to search the house," I said. "I certainly can't give them my testimony."

"What testimony? Did you—"

"Don't worry. I won't break and enter," I said, then swallowed the words, "this time."

"Did you say, 'this time?'"

"And it's getting icy. So, I'll just stick around here. If Vicki calls you, don't answer."

"I never do." He paused to add a string of curses. His voice sounded tinnier than Vicki's. Maybe it was my reception and not Fiji's. "Now listen. I'm speaking partner-to-partner here. You don't have back up. We don't know if Jim and Krystal are dangerous, but we do know Jim's been convicted of armed robbery. You're smart, and you're resourceful, kid. But you're getting in over your head. Again. We have no right to go into that woman's house unless she invites us. And you have no right to put yourself in danger. Again."

"That last part didn't make sense. Why would that be a right?"

"Do not put yourself in danger. Is that more clear?"

"Nash—"

"Dammit, Maizie. Just stay put in the neighbor's house. For once, can't you just wait it out?"

"What if Pearl's in danger? And Martha Mae?"

"And what about you? If they're in danger and you go sneaking into that house, you're in danger too. You make me half crazy, thinking of all the—" His voice shook. His breath expanded. Or was that wind?

"I'll be careful, don't worry."

"Of course, I'm worried. You do these—I wanted to spend Christmas Eve with you. I mean, Lamar spends it with his family. And I… so I just thought…never mind. That has no bearing on the issue. The point is, don't be stupid and get yourself hurt. Or killed. And if the roads are icy, yes, stay off them. Stay there. In a motel." He paused. "I'm done."

My heart did a Parkour leap up my throat, dove to my toes, and bounced back into my chest. "Oh my gosh. You don't want to be alone for Christmas Eve. You want to spend it with me. That is so sweet."

"Let's focus on what's important."

"That is so important, Nash. That's the point of every single Hallmark Christmas movie. And everyone loves those movies. Micky tried to get me an audition for *I'll be Home*— Okay, rule number one. No talking about my former career." I took a deep breath. "Focusing."

It was super hard to focus after hearing that. But business before pleasure, like Vicki always said.

With Vicki, we never got to pleasure. I'd hoped it'd be different with Nash.

"Bank robbery or not, call the police," said Nash. "Be concise as possible. But detailed. But only detail the facts."

"Got it."

"Then stay at the neighbor's house and watch Martha Mae's. Do not leave the house."

"Uh…"

"Miss Albright."

"I need to call you back," I said. "A car's slowing down in front of Martha Mae's house."

13 CHERRY TUCKER

I'D FORCED myself against the grogginess and haze to evaluate what I knew against what I thought I knew. Mrs. Boyes had disappeared from view. Whether she'd hurt her back or had been strangled by Santa was yet to be determined. Pearl had gone over there and not returned. She could be helping Mrs. Boyes. Or something else had happened.

Then the nephew — Santa? — had moved Mrs. Boyes's tree. Mrs. Boyes who hadn't touched the tree in all the Christmases I remembered visiting Great Gam. Nor the Christmases after moving into Great Gam's in-town home from Grandpa's farm. Mrs. Boyes wouldn't abide the changing any of her decorations, let alone a tree. She made the exact same cookies every year. Unfortunately. Hung the same wreath on her door.

Then this man had threatened my pregnant sister. That angered me beyond belief.

At that thought, the ice melted from my toes. Heat poured off my neck. Who was this supposed nephew? Pearl wasn't here to answer that question. I wasn't sending Casey over there to ask. Then I remembered Pearl had said Gertie Sweetly was Martha Mae's best friend. I didn't know Gertie Sweetley, but she'd know me. Everyone in Halo over the age of fifty-five knew me through my grandparents.

And through stories about my notorious mother. And maybe some stories about notorious me.

This was all confirmed when Gertie Sweetley realized who was calling. "Cherry Tucker, the town council has already chosen someone to paint the water tower. We have to use a professional company who's licensed and insured. And we don't want some gewgaw painted on the side. It's a rust-proof, army-gray type of job."

"Ma'am. That's not what I'm calling about—although something as tall as a water tower would be a fine place to represent town pride, but if y'all feel Halo is only worth army gray, then enjoy. I'm calling about your friend and my neighbor, Mrs. Boyes. She's got some strange visitors."

Gertie Sweetley snorted. "And even if we were to paint an angel on the water tower, you'd give us one of those abstract messes. Or worse. I know about those nekkid men paintings you did. Angels wear robes."

I sighed. "Miss Gertie. I really don't want to paint an angel on the water tower. And even if I did, it wouldn't be a nude. Even though nudes happen to be a classic representation of the human form used in art for longer than three thousand years."

"They never painted angels nekkid. I can tell you that for sure."

"I'm not arguing with you, Miss Gertie. Nude lends itself more to gods and goddesses. Although Michelangelo seemed to enjoy it in Biblical representation." I gave into a fit of coughing. She was wearing me out, and I hadn't even gotten to the point of the conversation. "I really just want to ask you about Mrs. Boyes's nephew who's visiting."

"Martha Mae doesn't have a nephew visiting."

"There's a man in her house who says he's her nephew."

"Oh, my stars," said Gertie. "A surprise Christmas guest. I wonder if she stocked up before this weather hit. Is that why you're calling? Does she need something? I bet she didn't buy a turkey. But why wouldn't Martha Mae call me if she needed a turkey? Anyway, I don't have an extra turkey, and I'm not running out to the Tru-Buy in this weather. Besides, the Tru-Buy is out of turkeys. She needs to go to Line Creek. The Winn Dixie is still stocked."

I closed my eyes, leaned back against my bed rails, and stared up at Snug. He was bathed in multi-colored lights, like the shrine on the wall at the nail salon. "Miss Gertie. Ma'am. I just want to know about Martha Mae's nephew."

"Don't tell me you're planning on cozying up to her nephew. I thought you were stepping out with JB's stepson? The deputy. And with him involved in this awful mess in town. Are you not seeing him no more? That poor man. But maybe it's for the best."

I opened my mouth and shut it before I said something I regretted. "I am not looking for a date, Miss Gertie. This nephew is old enough to be my father anyway. I am concerned that he is not a good sort. He moved Mrs. Boyes's tree."

"No, he didn't."

"He did. In front of her side window."

"Martha Mae wouldn't allow such a thing. She always places it in that corner opposite the front window so everyone can see her tree but not block the window, so she can see out. Martha Mae thought a lot about the tree placement over the years. She's tried it centered on the opposite wall, but then it interferes with the placement of her couch and she likes to watch her shows in the evening. Plus, you shouldn't put a live tree near a fireplace. That's asking for trouble."

"Exactly. Which is why I want to know who this so-called nephew is."

"I have no idea. But I can tell you this. He better not move any more of her things. She's not going to be happy when she finds her tree moved."

"Do you mean she's not at home? Do you know where Mrs. Boyes is?"

"No, hon'. But she can't be home if he's moved her tree, now can she?"

After hanging up, I watched Mrs. Boyes's tree lights blink and thought about the likelihood of Mrs. Boyes not being home. Casey had said her back was out. Maybe I should have mentioned that fact to Miss Gertie, but it was a road I didn't feel like exploring. Partly because the conversation exhausted me. And partly because I didn't want Miss Gertie getting any bright ideas about visiting her friend with the weather, bad roads, and Pearl already missing.

Come to think of it, Pearl would have told off the nephew for moving his aunt's tree, too.

The cost of the conversation was the creeping heat of fever. I shuddered with bone-aching chills and slid below my quilt. I pulled the quilt around my head and lay on my side, trying to analyze our conversation. Something else she'd said had bothered me. But now I couldn't remember. And it was getting difficult to stay awake again. I reached for my sketchbook to add a tree and Pearl, then closed my eyes for a minute.

Damn flu.

MY DREAMLESS SLEEP was interrupted by Casey, who claimed we'd have our own unexpected guest. The movie star. Who was as suspicious as Mrs. Boyes's nephew in my book.

I couldn't believe Casey had let that woman into my house. I couldn't stay awake for the life of me. And somewhere during my last slumber, Casey had invited the movie star to spend the night.

"The roads are iced over," Casey had said. "And Maizie's stuck. We can't let her sleep in her car. It's Christmas time, ain't it?"

"If it's that bad, I hope you're not planning to drive home," I said. "You take the guest bed, it's got a better mattress to support that extra weight you're carrying. The movie star can have my room. But we'll have to change the sheets."

Casey laughed at me. "She's fine with the couch. I've got Great Gam's plastic tree up, by the way."

Can you put it in here? I'd almost said, then caught myself. I'd almost forgotten I didn't do Christmas trees. "Keep it out there. Did you see Mrs. Boyes's bubble lights? You could take some pointers from her."

Then I'd fallen asleep. Again. I hated this flu. I was so damn weak it was pitiful.

After waking, I glared at glowing Snug. And then at Mrs. Boyes's tree, which I could see much better as it was pushed up against the window.

Also, something else was going on. Casey was acting extra nice. She didn't do extra nice. Even with child.

I tried calling Luke, but couldn't get through, figuring the bad roads must keep him extra busy. I didn't want him to see me like this. But then again, I really wanted to see him. He'd snuggle in bed next to me to rub my shoulders and stroke my hair. Tell me about all the accidents and arrests he'd handled. I loved cop stories. But mostly, I just wanted him here. For no apparent reason.

Damn flu making me addle-brained.

Casey appeared in my doorway with a steaming mug. "You want to try some chicken soup?"

My stomach rolled, but my mouth felt parched. "Maybe. What's the movie star doing?"

"She ain't a movie star. Maizie's a private investigator. I have her business card."

"Anybody can make a business card, Casey. Thank God we got nothing worth robbing in this house."

"I know you don't mean it," said Casey. "You're just worried about—"

"What am I worried about?" I squinted at her.

"Pearl," she spit out the name quickly. "And Mrs. Boyes.

Someone else showed up at her house. Maizie's gone over there to see who it is."

"Who does that kind of thing?" I took the mug and let the steam heat my face. "Sneaking around someone's house like that?"

"You, for one," said Casey. "On a number occasions. When you think somebody's up to something no good."

"Well, that's different." I sipped the soup and eased back, letting the savory heat trickle down my throat. My head wanted more, my stomach wasn't sure. "In those circumstances, I had evidence of criminal wrong-doing and was helping friends in need."

"That's exactly the same thing, except this Maizie is a professional. And you're not."

I gave Casey my best stink-eye.

She snorted. "What was that?"

I guess the illness had also weakened that effect.

"I found more boxes of Christmas lights," said Casey. "And there's a box in the guest room closet with your name. It also has decorations. Can I use them?"

"No." I chewed my lip. "Whatever. I'm too sick to care. There's a stocking in there that Grandma Jo made for me. You can have it for the baby."

"When's the last time you hung up that stocking?" Casey folded her arms. "Grandma Jo embroidered it with an angel carrying a paintbrush, right? I haven't seen that in years."

"Fifteen. I thought I was too old for Santa."

"Fifteen is how old you were when Grandma Jo died."

I looked up at the lights wrapped around Snug. "You can use it this year. I'm sure Santa visits those in utero."

As soon as Casey had left, I wrapped the blankets around my shoulders, turned off the lights, and crept to the window. With their soft glow, Snug's Christmas lights held off the edge of complete darkness. Hanging across the room, they didn't hinder my ability to see out the window. I left them on. I didn't have much of a view with the Christmas tree blocking Mrs. Boyes's living room.

But the glow from her house lights still illuminated the window, creating a hazy spotlight on the winter wonderland outside. And I could see a shape, crouching on the ground at the corner of Mrs. Boyes's house. The shape appeared to be watching the front of the house. Movie Star. Getting herself into trouble, likely.

I crossed back to get my mug of chicken soup. I needed to get over this flu fast. She was going to need my help.

#BabyItsColdOutside #ReallyCold #ReallyReallyCold

THE ARTIST'S drive was on the opposite side of the house from Martha Mae's. I had to leave the house and cross to Martha Mae's to see anything. The wind had died down, but the air felt thin and sharp. Woodsmoke from nearby fireplaces stung my lungs, but I also tasted wet pine from the surrounding trees. Casey had lent me another pair of mittens, which helped. A little. I felt like I'd never feel warm again.

If I'd been thinking I would have borrowed Carol Lynn's DeerNose weather apparel. Smelling like deer pee would be the least of my worries now. Frostbite, yes. Also, the camo would have come in handy with all this prowling.

Next time I see Daddy, I might advise him on a Christmas camouflage collection. Maybe poinsettias and holly? And to skip the scent. Deer don't celebrate Christmas.

A car, a Toyota sedan, had inched along the street, fishtailed, and slowed to a crawl as it reached Martha Mae's. The Toyota now idled behind Martha's parked car. Had Krystal finally showed?

I felt and heard the rumble of the garage door. My heart pounding, I backed from the edge of the house and flattened against the wall. Hearing nothing more than the garage door and the still-running car, I peeked around the corner.

Jay tramped into view. With a scraper, he chipped off ice then entered Mrs. Boyes's Buick. He backed into the grass, around the idling car, and parked on the street. Exiting the car, he shoved his hands in his pockets and tread up the drive. Stopping at the visitor's car, he leaned in. The car's window rolled down and the murmur of voices hung in the still air. It looked like a single driver. A moment later, Jay turned to face the house.

I shrank back against the wall.

Maybe another relative was coming to take care of Martha Mae. So nice, right? No doubt, Pearl was in the bedroom with her. Too busy applying hot compresses to talk. I could go back to the artist's house and drink hot chocolate with her pregnant sister. Their house might be chilly and leaky, but it wasn't the ice bath I felt out here.

"Yeah right." Julia Pinkerton sneered. "Here's how this is going down. You need to get inside that garage to look around. Then you can get inside the house. Keep low. Nobody's watching. I've done this a million times. Which means you've done it a million times, acting as me on the show."

"Are you insane?" I thought. "That wasn't even real. The writers made sure you weren't killed. There are no writers in real life."

Oh, my God, I was the one who's insane. Arguing with a fictional character inside my head.

Taking a deep breath, I peered around the edge of the house. The waiting car pulled into the garage. Jay followed, stomping and rubbing his hands together. Martha Mae's car remained on the street.

I held my breath, stood, and sidled around the edge of the

house. With my heart pounding in my head, I darted across the front yard. Ducked as I crossed before the porch. Before reaching the drive, I leaped behind a bush next to the garage.

This was the stupid Nash had spoken of. So stupid.

Keeping my back against the house, I glanced inside the garage. Two cars. The visiting vehicle plumed exhaust and cut off. The car door opened, but the driver had bent into the passenger seat to retrieve something. Jay circled the car and stopped at the back.

I dropped to the icy, wet ground, sliding to hide my body beneath the hedge. A holly. Prickly. And full of berries. Under the holly, fallen leaves rustled and rattled. I halted my slide. My shoulders and chest didn't fit beneath the shrub. If Jay and the other driver stepped outside the garage, they'd see me, lying Sphinx-like beneath a holly.

What was it with me and bushes today?

Someone was speaking. A woman. I didn't dare peer around the side of the garage.

"Unlock it," said Jay, followed by a thump.

"What're you doing?" called the woman's voice. "I told you it's not your business."

Did he want her to open the trunk?

A metallic pop and a creak answered that question.

"Shee-it," Jay muttered. "Why'd you get stuck with this mess? And now we're stuck here. Damn ice."

I held my breath and clamped my jaw to keep my teeth from chattering. My flattened stomach shot flames into my chest. Warming as well as painful. Cranking my head, I could just see the opposite edge of the garage. A pair of men's boots faced the car.

The trunk door slammed shut. "I'll take care of this mess. As usual."

"Don't give me that crap," said the woman. "I've been taking care of myself long enough. And done pretty good with what I've been dealt, I'd say."

A tremor worked its way through my legs. My shoulders shook, making the metal zipper on my coat jingle. Ducking, I placed my forehead on the corner of the drive to push my chest against the ground and stop the noise.

"Fine way to spend Christmas," said Jay.

"Right." Her forced laugh sounded brittle. "Because our other ones were so great."

"What were you doing asking Celia about Martha Mae? You put her on our tail. Celia sent a woman down here, and she's asking questions."

"We'll be gone soon enough."

"We ain't going anywhere with this ice. And we don't need you getting hot-headed again."

"I don't need *your* advice, of all people," said Krystal. "I've been doing just fine on my own."

The woman had talked to Celia Fowler. She must be Krystal. I found myself feeling pity for Krystal. She was a product of her upbringing.

"You can't get yourself out of this without my help," said Jay. "You wouldn't have called me otherwise."

"What do you want? A thank you note? You know what you're getting from this."

"I thought you were headed in the right direction for once," said Jay. "I told you to steer clear of her."

"Had no choice."

Who was her? Mrs. Fowler? But Krystal only took money from her grandmother. She didn't steer near her grandmother at all.

Unless her grandmother hadn't told us the truth. That thought made my chest hurt. It felt the equivalent to Vicki's "Let's talk about Santa and who really buys the toys around here" speech.

"Well, now I ain't got a choice either, do I?" Jay's boots clomped, stopping near my edge of the garage. "I couldn't do you right back then, I'll have to do you right now."

"Whatever."

I slithered backward, pushing myself into the corner of the house and garage.

A car alarm bloop-bleeped followed by another heavy, metallic pop. A trunk opening. Jay was checking the other trunk. A moment later the lid slammed shut. Boots tromped toward the far end of the garage. The garage door rumbled. An inside door slammed shut.

Scooting closer to the garage, I peered around the side. Flattening on the drive, I peered beneath the descending door. A woman walked toward the back of the garage. In a bulky coat and hat that hid her completely.

The garage door clanged against the cement, sending a cloud of dust into my face.

RETREATING to my holly bush corner, I regrouped. I needed to be certain that the newcomer was Krystal. But I really needed to find Pearl for the neighbors. And Martha Mae for myself.

I could watch from inside the artist's house like I'd promised Nash. Except I wouldn't be able to see anything. Sorry, Nash.

Stretching, I noted my silver jacket had gone camo. Streaks of brown and orange mud covered my puffy coat, pants, and boots. Private investigator work was so hard on my wardrobe. I tried not to think of the cost of my Gianvito Rossi boots. At least I had chosen leather over suede.

"Cheer up," I thought. "The Rossi's were last year's design anyway. Remember the distressing fad a few years back? Maybe mud camo will trend."

I feared my trending days were over. My shopper at Barney's would be so disgusted with me.

Biting my lip, I continued around the garage. On the back side of the house, I glanced at the unlit bushes (sorry Martha Mae), then studied the backyard. Martha Mae had a small, fenced vegetable garden. In the distance, a copse of trees hid the house from the neighbors' yard behind her. A screened-in porch decorated with boughs, lighted stars, and tiny Christmas trees flanked this end.

Lights were on in the kitchen, seen through the porch. Figures moved, but the porch blocked the view. There was a smaller window, set higher than the bedroom windows, probably placed above the kitchen sink. I was tall enough to peer through it, but I'd have to get close to the house and possibly expose myself. I'd have a better view of the kitchen on the porch. But a much greater chance of getting caught.

Kitchen sink, it was.

Creeping along the house, I thought I heard the muffled sounds of an argument. Arguments made my stomach clench, but so did sneaking around houses. It's a good sign, I told myself. Jay and She-Who-Might-Be-Krystal would be preoccupied with the dispute.

However, they'd also have heightened emotions. Which, if spotting someone skulk outside their house, might cause a rash action. For example, they might call the police.

Or try to hurt me.

I increased my speed around the screened porch and darted beneath the window. I rose slowly, angling to keep my body on the side of the window. From the side, I saw a door, a fridge, and part of another doorway. Martha Mae had a cute chicken border and oak cabinets. I ducked below the window and popped up on the other side. Someone sat a kitchen table, but they were blocked by Jay's large body. With his back to me (Hallelujah), he stood in a wide-legged stance. Arms folded. Immobile. Go figure, if they were still arguing.

The person at the table was shouting. A woman, judging by her arms. The only body parts I could see, unfortunately. The arms moved, pointing toward one end of the house and the other.

I pressed my ear against the wood frame, hoping to hear something useful, but could only make out the rise and fall of her voice. Occasionally, her high pitch was cut off by a low murmur. Which I took as Jay's response.

Not a very talkative guy. Kind of a one-sided argument.

Jay swung around. I sucked in my breath and shrank back against the house. His eyes, dark and angry, had darted toward the window.

OMG, had he seen me? My heart pounded. Blood rushed inside my ears. I couldn't move.

Water turned on. Jay had to be standing at the sink. He spoke again, a low rumble muffled by the water. The water turned off. A door slammed. The wall behind me vibrated.

I pivoted slowly, inching toward the window. Scooted back at the sound of a second door slamming. Took a deep breath. And peeked.

The woman had disappeared from view. Jay stomped through the kitchen carrying a bag and a shovel. A big one. With a pointy end. He cut around the kitchen table and out of my view. Metal scraped, and something heavy dragged, then rolled.

Craptastic. The sliding glass door. He was coming outside. My heart leaped into my throat. I pulled away from the window and flattened against the wall. Had he seen me? Was he coming to knock my head in with a shovel?

Jay slammed the sliding door shut, making the wall behind me shudder. Inside the screened porch, he used the shovel to knock down Martha Mae's little trees. Swiped at the lighted stars swinging from the porch rafters. Littered the ground with tiny ornaments.

Pressed against the wall, I fought off shudders. Poor Martha Mae. All her decorating work ruined with a few swings of a shovel. I tried not to think what the shovel also might do to my head. Jay hadn't given an indication that he knew I was out here. But he would see me if I ran.

He'd see me if I didn't run. I felt like crying. The thought of frozen snot kept back the tears.

Taking a break from his Christmas demolition, Jay shoved

open the screen door on the opposite side of the porch. It swung back and crashed into the frame. With a final swipe at an angel hanging above the door, he lumbered into the yard.

Slowly, I sank toward the ground. Keeping my back to the wall, I sat on my haunches in a tight huddle, hoping the shadows would keep me hidden. Above me, the light from the kitchen shone through the window.

Jay tromped through the icy grass, the bag swinging from one hand, the shovel dragging behind him. It made an eerie ringing, cutting across the cold, bumpy ground. At Martha Mae's garden, he unlatched and opened the gate, more carefully than he'd done on the porch. Dropping the bag on the ground, he began to dig. Jay strained against the frozen top layer. His labored breathing grew louder with his muttered curses. Eventually, the sound of shovel hitting clay and the flung dirt smacking the frozen garden became rhythmic.

I couldn't move. I needed to move. Jay was preoccupied. There was a chance he wouldn't see me. The front half of the garden fence had lights hanging from it. I could see him, he probably couldn't see me.

There was also a chance he could see me. And he had a big, wicked shovel. Plus, he was making a very large hole in the ground.

For a body?

My thighs shook. My knees felt close to exploding. Cold had set into my bones.

A new fear. Frozen joints. I'd be permanently stuck in this crouch like an overlarge, frosty garden gnome. Jay would find me, pick me up like he was carrying a super-sized pretzel, and toss me in the hole. They'd find my skeleton, bones contorted and fused together, and wonder what monster had been buried in Halo years before.

I didn't want the fate of an unwanted garden gnome.

Summoning all my courage and Julia Pinkerton's swagger (nine years younger, she was also lithe and flexible) I kept my back against the house and crab-walked. With the speed of a large, ancient tortoise. At the corner of the house, I slithered. One appendage, then the next. Dropped on all fours. And crawled until I felt more safely out of sight. Did a quick round of cow to cat yoga to loosen my muscles, pushed into downward dog to relieve my calves, and unfolded (slowly, creakingly) to upright. I leaned against the house wall, panting.

Felt a little better. Except for feeling like an idiot.

Jay was burying something in Martha Mae's kitchen garden. Guns? A stash of bank money? Bodies?

And what was I going to do? My plans had gone from convincing Krystal to return home to visit her Grandma, to doing what? Saving two elderly ladies from possible bank robbers? Who shot people and kidnapped cops? Come on. Even Julia Pinkerton didn't do stuff like that on the show. Nobody had guns. They mostly shot off their mouths. The writers couldn't risk a rating censure.

I ambled forward, stopping at Martha Mae's living room window. Her Christmas tree blocked the view into the house. I stared at the bubbling and blinking lights for a moment and listened to the distant ring of shovel on dirt.

Big hole.

What if it was for a body?

Yanking off my hat, I ran my fingers through my hair, then caught myself in the window's reflection. Someone I didn't know looked back at me. Her eyes had a hard, calculating set to them. Her former Colgate smile had vanished for a grim scowl. And let's not talk about the woman's hair. I did not want to go there. I pulled the beanie back on.

I'd always been impetuous — borderline reckless — but more like, the imprudent "rich kid from Beverly Hills" type. That was embarrassing enough to admit. I couldn't save anybody from bank robbers. Not when the bank robber might shoot them. Or me. What would that do to Daddy? Find out his daughter was shot at Christmas? And Remi? I'd promised her I'd be home for

Christmas Eve. I'd ruin Vicki's Fiji holiday. I didn't have high hopes for getting her a bikini in time, but no chance of that now if I was dead.

Also, Nash. He wanted to spend Christmas Eve with me, too. I was more excited about that than a visit from Santa.

Plus, Nash would kill me if I got shot.

I RAN (SLID) to Tiffany's car and laid flat on the back bench seat. For a long moment, I stared at the ceiling, panted, and wiggled my numb toes. I assumed Jay continued his (literal) skullduggery and the-woman-I-presumed-was-Krystal did whatever she deemed necessary after a bank robbery (Showered? Counted money? Renewed her passport?).

"You don't know for sure they're bank robbers," I told myself. "Possibly, this is all one big mistake. They're visiting Aunt Martha Mae (who they'd never visited previously) to help her with her back. And Jay is digging a coffin-shaped hole in her garden because people with bad backs shouldn't be digging."

"Yeah, right," said my inner Julia Pinkerton. "That hole is *for* Martha Mae."

I was in way over my head. I had to call the police. As soon as they showed to protect the sick artist and her pregnant sister, I'd drive to the twenty-four-hour Waffle Hut, spend the night in a booth, and drive home in the morning. Surely in the morning, the sun would come out, melt the ice, and I'd be on the road with plenty of time to binge-watch all the Rankin-Bass Christmas shows with Remi. She went to bed early. I'd have time to see Nash. Did he have an office Christmas party planned? Would we drink eggnog and do a Secret Santa exchange? Mistletoe in his office door?

Kind of hard to do Secret Santa with two people. Maybe he'd include Lamar. Hopefully not Jolene Sweeney, because that's a sure way of knowing I'd get coal. But if Lamar and Jolene were invited, I doubted there would be mistletoe.

Hello, Maizie. No secret Santa until I knew these people were safe.

I dialed 9-1-1.

"9-1-1. What's your emergency?"

Nash had said concise but detailed. But detail only the facts.

"Possible violence," I answered. "I don't think you'd call it a domestic, but it is in a domestic domicile. 213 Loblolly. Martha Mae Boyes's house. Not Martha Mae. I don't think she'd hurt a fly. I'm not positive, but her nephew and grandniece might be armed. Possibly they're bank robbers? In any case, I'm concerned for Martha Mae and Pearl. I don't know Pearl's last name. She raises goats? Also for her neighbors, Cherry and Casey. I forgot their last names. One is sick, and the other is pregnant. We're talking the endangerment of the elderly and the infirm. Not that pregnancy is an illness. Casey looked pretty healthy to me. In any case, we haven't heard from Martha Mae or Pearl for quite a while. They could be held hostage."

"Your name, please?"

"Maizie— Does it matter?" I said, thinking of my probation officer and her hearty dislike of my job. "I'm just visiting."

"Visiting Cherry Tucker?" The voice hardened. "Did Cherry tell you to call?"

"No. I'm supposed to be visiting Martha Mae? But she never came to the door? Just the nephew. And he's a convicted felon. Although he served his time. His daughter is out after an arrest. But she wasn't charged with anything."

"And you saw them with weapons? Did you say they're armed?"

"Not totally sure on that point? But I know the bank robbers are armed."

"Have you heard any gunshots? Any evidence they're using the weapons?"

"No."

"Where are you now? I'll send an officer out to talk to you."

"In a car…" I chewed my lip.

"What's your business there?"

"Martha Mae's sister sent me to talk the grandniece into coming home for Christmas?" My nerves were making me uptalk. This was not going well. I sounded crazy. "I heard about the bank robbers and…"

"Yes, we've gotten a lot of calls about the bank robbers today. I'll send an officer to speak to you—"

"I'm leaving. I need to get home." All I needed was for a Halo deputy to look me up and learn I'm on probation. And contact my probation officer. Who was scary. "Can the officer just go to Martha Mae's house and check on her?"

"They'd like to talk to you first."

"I've got to get home," I said. "Never mind me. Just send someone out to keep an eye on Martha Mae's. And the house next door, 211 Loblolly. I'm worried they're not safe. The officer needs to make sure Martha Mae and Pearl are okay. Pearl went to check on Martha Mae, and she hasn't come back."

"Thank you for your information. As soon as an officer is available, they'll be there. The roads are bad, so please wait. Remain where you are so they can speak to you. Are you at the house?"

"No." I hung up.

Craptastic. I lowered my head to the steering wheel and jerked back. Freezing cold and with me sweating bullets, I might have stuck. That's all I needed, my forehead stuck to a steering wheel. Finding a candy cane in my pocket, I pulled back the plastic on the end that wasn't covered in tape and shoved it in my mouth. I needed sugar in a very bad way.

My therapist Renata and my trainer Jerry would be so disappointed. One for needing a crutch and the other for eating chemically treated high-fructose corn syrup. Jerry said I might as well eat poison.

I'd take candy cane poison over getting killed any day.

Sucking on the candy cane, I stared out the window. In the artist's house, the pregnant sister was decorating a small tree she'd placed in the window. That looked normal. Pleasant. Christmas-y. Giving me hope that this was all just some crazy storm of coincidences that meant nothing.

Why did I agree to help Mrs. Fowler? She was a terrible grandmother.

Granted I didn't know that at the time. Nor was I even sure about that now.

At Martha Mae's, there was movement. I squinted and fast-sucked my candy cane. The door opened. Light spilled onto the porch.

Oh, my God. Jay was leaving the house again. Did he finish digging? Was he coming here? Was the hole for me? I slid halfway down my seat, keeping my eyes on Jay.

Using Martha Mae's porch posts, Jay banged the mud off his shoes. I hated to think what he'd done to poor Martha Mae's floors. I took the candy cane from my mouth, pulled the plastic over the now-sharp end, and shoved it in my pocket. My heart beat in my throat.

Still on the porch, Jay lit a cigarette. Slowly, he scanned the street.

I dropped beneath my window. Blood pulsed inside my ears. I felt dizzy. Realized I was panting again. Deliberately slowed my breathing.

At least my puffing made the car smell minty.

I wanted to look up, but fear kept me crouched beneath the seat. Possibly Jay was taking a smoke break. Rewarding himself after the hard work. Hard work of burying bodies.

Santa, I want a patrol car for Christmas. Early. Like right now. With flashing lights and a siren.

I peeked through the driver's window. Jay was no longer on the porch. I inched my way up the door, peering right and left. Climbed onto the seat. No Jay.

A tiny orange light between the houses winked and went out. Was that Jay? In his neighbor's yard? The sick artist's house.

Hells. What was he doing there? Did they have a garden for burying bodies, too?

I quietly opened the door and set a foot on the road. My boot slid sideways. I hit the road with both hands. Bit my lip to keep from crying out. Kicked the door shut and crawled forward. Prayed no one would drive down the street and splatter me. At the artist's driveway, I pushed up, slid toward the Firebird and hand-over-hand, vehicle-by-vehicle, trekked up the driveway. In the carport, I ran to the kitchen door and stopped.

I didn't want to freak out a pregnant woman and someone sick with the flu. I knocked. Quietly.

Casey appeared. I sidled past her and shut the kitchen door.

"Did you find Pearl?" she said.

"Not yet." I didn't want to tell her what I did find. "I just wanted to let you know that I'm going to be checking out your yard? Just ignore me? But, maybe stay away from the windows and lock your doors?"

"What in the hell is going on?"

"I'm being cautious. Checking the perimeters. But maybe get out your sister's gun and stay in that room with her?" I opened the kitchen door, shut it behind me. The lock clicked.

I was alone in their yard. With Jay. Again.

Worst Christmas ever.

15   CHERRY TUCKER

MY EYES FELT tight and dry. My head foggy and full. I shook with chills. But while Casey busied herself decorating for the Christmas I didn't want to have, I had pulled on layers to free my body of blankets and positioned myself before the window.

I'd seen Santa. Creeping around my house.

Casey didn't need to know. She'd fight me, knowing I was out of bed, let alone what I planned on doing. Luke wouldn't call me back, which told me the sheriff's office was in over their heads between the weather and the domestic disturbances that always happened this time of year. If I called the dispatcher, she'd just think the flu had melted my brain. Besides, I had nothing much to report other than a tree that had been moved and two missing women who might just be watching *A Charlie Brown Christmas* rerun in Mrs. Boyes's bedroom.

I'd unplugged Snug's lights, darkening the room, and half-hid against the wall. The light next door gave the nephew away, but even in the shifting shadows, the glowing end of a cigarette drifted near his face. He'd strolled around the edge of the house. Stopped in the corner of Mrs. Boyes's house, where he dragged on the cigarette then let his arm drop and hang. Facing my house. Like he was studying it.

My eyes narrowed. I no longer felt the chill. Heat poured off me, damp and angry. My sister and her baby were in my house. And this man had threatened her. For what? Watching our Pearl argue with him through his aunt's window? What was he hiding with that tree? And where the hell was Pearl?

I wanted in that house. But I couldn't leave Casey alone with Creepster Santa hanging outside my window. A light knock in the kitchen startled me. Creepy nephew was still standing next to his aunt's house, smoking. I left him to sneak down the hallway and peer into the kitchen.

The movie star was back. Casey had let her in. Dammit. It was going to be harder for me to sneak out with the prying eyes of the so-called PI in the house. But then, she'd keep an eye on Casey while I could see what the nephew was doing.

I swiped at the sweat dampening my neck and listened.

What in the hell? Movie Star knew about Pearl? And she was checking our perimeter? Did she know the nephew was out there? Idiot. She'd get herself into trouble. That one did not look capable of taking on a killer Santa.

If the nephew had strangled Mrs. Boyes with Christmas lights. I still wasn't sure.

But Movie Star was plenty worried about Pearl. I could hear it in her voice. She shook with tension. Or maybe with cold.

Why didn't Casey offer her a cup of cocoa or something?

She left. Movie Star was out there with creepy Santa.

It was time to pull out the Remington. For Casey and the baby's sake.

MY HAIR FELT SLICK with sweat and my hands clammy, but I ignored the fever. Keeping an eye on the window, I busied myself with a half-cocked — as Luke would call it — plan. After I had checked and filled the Remington with shells, I placed the shotgun on the guest bed. I'd make Casey spend the rest of the night in there. She and I had been raised with hunters. Casey knew her way around a shotgun. Anyway, Uncle Will had made us take gun safety classes every year. His responsibility as sheriff, he'd said.

In my bedroom, I had plugged the Christmas lights back in and piled my pillows beneath the blanket. From the outside, if anyone cared to peek in my window, it'd look like I was sleeping. Found the trigger and door stop alarms Luke had gotten from a home security seminar. Then pulled out the lights from Great-Gam's box of Christmas decorations and took a moment to admire the thick wiring and heavy duty bulbs.

I had a few surprises set up for Santa. Just in case he tried to come down my chimney early this year.

While I stretched Christmas lights between eye-screws, the ping-pong of my front doorbell startled me. Casey, still working on the tree, answered. She kept her voice hushed, but I recognized the fear in her rushed whisper. Whoever was there, she wouldn't allow in the house.

Dumping the lights, I leaped into the guest room, grabbed the Remington, and half-slid down my hall. Tearing around the arched doorway, I ran into the living room.

"Get out of the way, Casey." I racked the shotgun and swung it up to my shoulder, pressing my cheek against the stock. "Whoever you are, I am armed, and this gun is loaded."

Casey cried out and spun around, hugging her belly. A man stepped into the doorway and shoved her aside. A handgun rose, pointed at me.

"Drop your weapon," he yelled. "Police."

"Cherry, it's Deputy Fells," called Casey. "What in the hell are you doing? Please don't shoot her, Fells. She's crazy with fever."

My finger slid off the trigger guard. Raising my left hand, I bent to lay the Remington on the floor. "I thought you were the creepy nephew." My voice faltered. "Oh, Lord forgive me. I swear on my life, I would never knowingly aim a gun at law enforcement, Jake."

Clouds swam across my vision. I felt, more than saw, Casey at my side, walking me to the sofa.

"You should've stayed in bed. You shouldn't be out here." Casey glanced behind her. "Jake, why don't we talk on the porch?"

"You sure?" The deputy looked up from his squat, the Remington in his arms.

"No," I yelled. "All y'all, stay inside. He's out there. Santa. He's watching the house."

"What?" Jake popped a cartridge from the shotgun, checked for the next round, and looked up. "Was that your call, Cherry? I know you've got the flu, but you've got to stay off the lines. We're still on a manhunt and the roads are terrible. We're making shitty progress."

"Call? Cherry called?" Casey's voice sounded sharp. "Fells, I thought you were coming out here to tell us about Luke— Never mind. Let me get Cherry to bed, and we'll talk."

"Luke?" I said. "Why would you come here to tell us about Luke?"

The heat drained from my body. Cold seeped in, turning my fingers white. I stared at my hands, then at Casey.

A fat tear rolled down her cheek. She swiped at it, raised her chin, and looked away.

"What happened?" I turned toward Fells.

His body vibrated with tension. Pulling the action bar back on the Remington, he popped out another round and set the cartridge on the floor. Keeping his eyes on the shotgun, he continued to unload it.

"Fells, I'm really sorry. I didn't know it was law enforcement at the door. What manhunt? Where's Luke? Is he on the manhunt?"

The deputy's jaw twitched. His eyes moved from the shotgun to Casey. Lines had tightened around his eyes as he switched his gaze back to me. "You can't go waving a gun around, Cherry. What if I were a neighbor kid? I could call you in on that."

"Please don't make this worse," said Casey. "It's already bad enough."

"I know. I'm sorry. I'm really sorry," I said. "I thought someone was threatening Casey and the baby. I have to protect her."

Casey clamped a hand over her mouth. Her eyes squeezed shut, and tears bled from the corners. Sniffing, she lifted her hand. "I know you have to tell his family first," she said, her voice a raw whisper. "But can't you tell us something?"

"I don't know anything for sure, Casey. I can't tell you what I don't know." Holding the shotgun, Deputy Fells rose. Shotgun shells stood in a row at his feet. "What's Cherry talking about?"

She sighed. "The weird neighbor next door caught me watching him through the window, and he gave me the finger across the throat sign."

Fells held up a hand and backed out the doorway. After leaning to look at the house next door, he stepped back inside. "Your neighbor did that? Who lives there?"

"Martha Mae Boyes. Not her. Her nephew." Casey rubbed her eyes with the back of her arm. "Martha Mae hurt her back. Her nephew is creeping us out."

"You want me to talk to him?"

"Forget it." She shook her head. "You better tell us what you know."

Dazed, I looked from Deputy Fells to Casey. I couldn't stop shaking. A pit had formed inside my chest. Afraid of what would fall in, I shouted, "Tell him about Pearl."

Casey spoke woodenly. "Pearl went over to check on Martha Mae and hasn't come back."

"Did you call her?" asked Fells.

"Of course, we called her. She didn't answer," I said. "And I called Gertie Sweetley."

"I'm taking away your phone," snapped Casey. "Why can't you just rest in bed like a normal person?"

"I'm not normal," I yelled. My voice broke. A lump rose in my throat, and I thought I might choke. "Go next door, Jake Fells. There's something going on. I saw Santa choking Mrs. Boyes with the Christmas lights."

"You did not," hissed Casey. "It's the fever. You got me all worked up, too. I didn't want to think about Luke, so I played along. Stop it. Just let Deputy Fells say what he's got to say. There's no point in waiting anymore."

"The nephew threatened you. You saw that." I gasped. My chest constricted. I couldn't catch a breath. "Pearl's over there. The nephew moved the tree. And Mrs. Boyes's car is on the street. Did you see that?"

"You think Grandpa wanted to hear Grandma Jo's cancer had come back? He listened to the doctor anyway, even though the doctor was an ass." Casey took another swipe at her tears. "I know it's Christmas. I've been trying to protect you from the news. But your man is a deputy. You know what can happen. Don't make this harder on Fells."

Fells had taken his hat off. Held it between his hands.

I slid back against the wall. My bones hurt too much to sit up. I nodded for him to continue while the pit inside me widened. I teetered at the edge, noting the darkness beneath.

Deputy Fells started with the bank robbery. Told me Luke was a hero. Explained the gang's escape and the reasons why they'd lost the van. Then lost the perps.

And lost my man.

Numbly, I took the last step and fell into that pit.

#FrostyTheSnowWoman

I HOPED Casey and her sick sister would be safe. Possibly, Jay had just picked a strange place to smoke. Nash would accuse me of jumping to conclusions. But he'd also say the situation was hinky at best.

From the artist's carport, I tiptoed to peer around the back of the house, but I couldn't see Jay nor the burning embers of his cigarette. The artist's backyard had a fence running around it. Unless he'd returned to Martha Mae's, Jay still watched from the side of her house.

In the artist's drive, I positioned myself between the old truck and the Firebird, squatting in the shadow between them. Spotted Jay still at the corner of Martha Mae's house, smoking. Innocently. Or smoking was a pretense for something else. Why would he stand on the side of the house in the freezing cold and not on the porch?

Was he watching the artist's house? Or waiting for someone?

After thirty minutes of squatting, I thought I'd lose my mind.

They don't teach you stuff like this in the Criminal Justice courses at U Cal, Long Beach. The temperature continued to drop. I couldn't feel my toes. Under the streetlight, the neighborhood yards looked coated in sugar. The street glistened and not in a good way. Beneath me, a thin layer of ice covered the cement. I had to remind myself that I'd have more heat loss standing than squatting. Silver Linings. However, I could see glute exercises in my future.

A depressing thought so close to Christmas.

I'd make it a New Year's resolution. I couldn't disappoint Carol Lynn by turning down all the cookies she'd spent weeks baking. Not to mention the holiday dinner she'd planned. There'd been a mention of green bean casserole. Which, I'm pretty sure, is illegal in California. Anyway, I'd never tasted it. But I liked any food with the word casserole in the title.

My Christmas dinner reflections were interrupted by a car's engine. The motor gunned and slackened in choppy repetition. Eventually, the vehicle appeared, creeping down the street. Sliding and recovering. A patrol car. Forks County Sheriff.

Hallelujah. The cavalry.

They didn't use lights and sirens, but Santa must have heard my prayer. Soon, this would all be over. The pregnant sister would tell the cop about the black hole in Martha Mae's house where people keep disappearing. They'd quickly figure out Jay and the woman-who-may-be-Krystal must be connected to the bank robbery, giving them the legal impetus to search the house.

(Unless, of course, Krystal turned out to be a nun, wrongly accused of a crime. The judge had dropped her earlier charges, after all. I still had hope for Krystal.)

But finally, I'd be warm. And I could make my way home to Remi and Nash. As soon as the roads cleared.

Julia Pinkerton never let the police take over a case unless she'd already solved it. That's the difference between TV fiction and real life. I was happy to turn over this mess to the cops. Nash would be proud of me. Not only did I find Krystal (I think), but I helped solve a bank robbery (maybe). I was too cold to pat myself on the back, but props is props.

If the police needed extra testimony, I'd crawl out of my hiding spot. For now, I (and, by default, my probation officer) would stay out of their way.

The poor deputy was having difficulty parking at the curb. The car kept sliding into the street. Oh boy, black ice.

Speaking of ice. I glanced at the sheen below me, hoping my boots hadn't stuck. Not that I was doing anything wrong, but it didn't seem smart to stay crouched between cars on someone's driveway with a police officer about to walk past me. I scrambled up the drive, grabbing vehicles to pull myself along. Under the carport, I crept toward the fence. Put my hand on the gate, changed my mind, and circled the outside of the fence.

Following the fence, I plodded along in the crunchy grass. Passing Martha's dug-up garden, I headed for the group of trees that hid her house from the neighbor's. It was too far to see anything well, but a good place to stakeout (or hide) while the police did their thing. I figured bank robbers trying to escape the police would run out the back of the house. The police would surround the house. I'd get to see the action from this safe vantage point.

And could melt into the backyard behind me if the action looked a little too hot.

For a good forty-five minutes, I waited, shivering next to a tree. A copse of trees is much colder than hunkering near a house. Tried calling Nash, but he didn't answer. Thought about calling Lamar, but he went to bed super early due to owning the Dixie Kreme Donut Shop. I stood then squatted, willing myself to think warm thoughts. Tried on a very merry Nash Christmas fantasy, but when he took off his shirt (in my head), I broke out in goosebumps, making the cold worse. Even the memory of his Jessica Rabbit tat flexing over his massive deltoid did nothing for me. Except wish Jessica into a sweater.

Throwing a blanket over the dream of near-naked Nash, I added a roaring fire. And a space heater.

I was having a blue Christmas. Literally. My fingers were going to fall off. My nose felt a shade similar to Santa's. I was pretty sure my internal organs had a coating of frost. No longer numb, my toes actually hurt. *The Shining's* ending kept flashing through my mind. Which didn't help me feel any warmer.

Forget it, I thought. I'd rather get in trouble with my probation officer than hide from the police. At least a California prison was warm.

I trudged across the backyard, angling toward the artist's house. On the way, I checked the garden where Jay had been digging. The string of lights provided enough illumination to see the hole had been filled in. Which was a little comforting. Also, a little disconcerting, not knowing what had been in the hole. I thought about a quick dig (one way to warm up), but the shovel was gone. I'd just point the police toward the lovely mound full of evidence Jay had left for them.

Nearing the artist's fence line, I halted to check the side of the house. Jay had disappeared. He'd seen the patrol car, obviously. I crept between the houses, hoping I didn't look as suspicious as I felt. Peered into the front yard.

No patrol cars. Not even one.

What happened to my cavalry? Had Jay been caught quickly and quietly and taken back to the sheriff's office? But wouldn't I have heard something? All was calm. Not so bright. I could see well enough into the house. Lights were on in the back, but there was no movement.

Wait. If the police hadn't arrested Jay…Or hadn't searched the house for bank robbers…Or missing people…

That meant I was the cavalry.

Supershizzles.

17 CHERRY TUCKER

FOR WHAT FELT like a long time, I couldn't make myself move from the settee. I lay slumped against the wall, feeling but not feeling the ache in my bones. I stared at the little tree Casey had put in the front window. Hating it. Hating the cheap ornaments and the blinkety-blink lights and the tacky gold tinsel she'd draped over the branches with little care. An end dangled from the bottom branch, swaying as the heater kicked on beneath it. Tiny bits of tinsel and fake pine needles vibrated on the wooden floor. She'd tacked my stocking to the window ledge. Grandma Jo's artist angel smiled at me.

I didn't smile back. I wanted to walk across the room and throw the tree out the door. Rip the stocking down. Once again Christmas had brought me nothing but pain and heartache. Even my quickie marriage and even quicker annulment from Todd had happened at Christmas. And this year I had the flu.

The damn pit inside me yawned, but I refused to think about *that*.

"You want anything, Cherry?" Casey called from the kitchen. "Tea?"

I wanted Christmas to be over. I wanted this flu to be done. I wanted Deputy Fells to believe me about Mrs. Boyes's creepy nephew. I wanted Pearl to stroll in and tell me she'd helped Martha Mae slip her disc back in place.

I wanted Luke back.

But I wasn't thinking about *that*.

Pushing myself into sitting, I considered the creepy nephew, Pearl, and Martha Mae. I shuffled into the kitchen. We'd waited too long to check on Pearl.

I'd waited too long. Damn flu.

"When exactly was the bank held up?"

"What?" Casey glanced over her shoulder. She stood at the stove, stirring a pot. Barefoot and pregnant.

I shook that thought from my mind. "What time was the bank robbed?"

"Around noon." She paused her stirring, then resumed to a furious whisking.

"Why didn't you tell me?" I hugged my arms across my chest to keep from shivering.

"I didn't want to ruin your Christmas."

"Too late for that." I couldn't keep the vehemence from my voice. "I already had the flu."

Her head dipped and body trembled. She turned slowly, fighting tears. "If it weren't the flu, it'd be something else. You're bound and determined to find something wrong with this time of year. And we have a lot to be thankful for."

"Not me. Not anymore." I stared at her belly, hating my argument. From inside the pit, I could only see dark walls.

She turned back to the stove. "I'm sorry I didn't tell you about the bank robbery. And…Luke. But you were laid flat—should be still—and I don't trust you. You've already been talking crazy today about what's going on next door—"

"Crazy? Pearl's not back, Case. Despite what Deputy Fells said, things are not right over there." My voice rose, and I forced myself back to calm. "That man's been acting weird all day. I know what I thought I saw. You telling me you're not worried about Pearl? You want to call Grandpa Ed and tell him that Pearl could be in trouble and we're doing nothing to help her?"

"Pearl can handle herself."

"You sure about that?"

Casey spun to face me. "She's over there helping Martha Mae. You've been delusional. Half of what you've said today has made no sense."

"We don't *know* that Martha's hurt her back. You tried to talk Deputy Fells out of going next door. It's his job, Casey."

Her bottom lip trembled. She wrapped her arms around her belly. "For the same reason you should have, too. Because he needs to be out there looking for Luke Harper's—"

"Don't you say it," I hissed. "Don't say body."

"If there's a situation next door, they'd pull deputies off the manhunt." Casey sniffed. "But you know procedure. Uncle Will lectures us on it enough. Procedure means even if they have probable cause, they need a warrant to search the house. And Fells did go next door. He didn't get invited inside, but he said he talked to Pearl himself."

"I don't believe him. Maybe the nephew threatened her or something. Why wouldn't Pearl answer her phone? And why's Mrs. Boyes's car parked on the street? They moved her tree and the car, Casey. It's weird."

"The nephew was with Mrs. Boyes when the robbery happened. The nephew's just creepy. Pearl's not in any trouble. She's staying with a sick friend."

"The nephew could be involved with the bank robbery."

"You're ridiculous."

My sister was ridiculous, too. But the hollows beneath her eyes were purplish-blue. Her shoulders had bowed like she'd wilted. Her normal cock-of-the-walk demeanor seemed more like scared hen.

Casey'd never been a Luke Harper fan. Hated his family and him by default. Motherhood had filled her with a crazed yearning to see me settled. And since she couldn't convince me to take back my sort-of-ex, Todd, she'd turned her hurry-up-and-get-my-sister-married sights on Luke. And now her heart was breaking for him. A man, seven months earlier, she'd claimed to hate.

Hormones. Rotting her brain and revving her emotions. Probably what drove Eve to take that damn apple.

"Why don't you lie down in the guest room?" I said. "I'm feeling better. I'll look after myself."

She yawned. "I'm making cocoa."

"You can reheat it later. Take a nap or something."

She didn't argue but shuffled toward the guest room.

I followed her, carrying the Remington. "I'll leave this with you. Be careful because it's loaded."

"I thought Fells unloaded it." Casey gave me a look but took the shotgun.

I strolled to the single window that looked onto the porch. Double-pane with built-in muntin bars and plantation shutters. Front-facing windows with a couple layers of wood and glass. It felt safer than my bedroom. The side windows on my house didn't have muntin bars. I locked the shutters with the hook and eye. Closed the louvers.

"Don't do anything stupid, Cherry."

I turned from the window. Casey stood cradling the shotgun over her belly.

"I'm not about to start stupid now," I said. "But keep the lights off, just in case. I've taken some security measures."

She arched an eyebrow and climbed into bed. "You're still sick."

"I'm being careful."

This wasn't my first rodeo, although it was my first with the flu. Maybe Casey had hoped Movie Star would take care of business. But who knows where the PI had gone.

It was time for me to get back in the saddle, flu be damned. I might have lost Luke, but I wasn't going to lose my sister and Pearl.

. . .

OUTSIDE, the cold just about knocked me over. Followed by the ice. I slip-slided my way to Mrs. Boyes's, glad I had bundled up. If I crashed, at least my layers would prevent the fall from hurting too much. On Mrs. Boyes's porch, I glanced in the front window, noted the empty room and the placement of the tree. The tree fueled my anger. Anger forestalled my flu symptoms. Shoving my finger into her buzzer, I rang long, then with repeated jabs.

Nothing.

I pounded on the door. "I know y'all are in there," I hollered, cupping my hand over my mouth and aiming my voice at the glass. "I demand to see Pearl."

Grabbing the doorknob, I rattled it. "I've no patience for this today."

I stomped to the steps, knelt, and lifted the poinsettia pot, looking for Mrs. Boyes's key. No key. Everyone knew Mrs. Boyes kept her key under that pot. Rage surged through me. First the tree, then the car, and now the key.

I kicked the door with my boot and hammered with my fist. "You know that deputy who was just here? Did you see him while y'all were slinking around my yard? I'll get the law back here. I'm giving you to the count of five before I dial 9-1-1. And if you're really related to Mrs. Boyes, you'd know my uncle is sheriff."

A light flipped on in the kitchen.

Figured.

A woman answered the door. Brunette with short hair.

That I wasn't expecting.

"Who're you?" she said.

"You're kidding me, right?" I said. "Because I know you don't live here. You've got no business asking me who I am. Who're you?"

"Martha Mae's niece."

"Miss Martha Mae doesn't have a niece." I narrowed my eyes. She narrowed hers back. "She damn well does. It's me."

"Then you can tell me your name. I've known Mrs. Boyes my whole life and she's never once mentioned a niece."

"It's Krys. I'm here for Christmas."

"Isn't that nice? Bless your heart." I scanned her slim body, looking for odd lumps that might indicate a weapon. If this were only summer. Krys wore a bulky sweater that halfway covered her jeans. No way to tell. "Krys, get out of my way. I need to talk to Pearl."

"Who's Pearl?" she said.

"Who's Pearl? The woman apparently taking care of Mrs. Boyes's alleged back condition. When she's supposed to be helping me get over the flu. Now if I find Pearl's caring for Miss Martha Mae, I'll mosey back home. But if something's happened to her, you're in for it."

"Am I?" she arched a brow. She placed a hand on the frame, blocking my passage.

"Don't mess with me," I snarled. "I'm infecting you with influenza as we speak. And it's the stomach kind. If you were smart, you'd get out of my way."

"If you were smart, you'd go home."

"No one's ever accused me of being a brain surgeon." I placed a hand on my hip. "But they do accuse me of being fearless." Also, foolhardy, but I wasn't going to add that. "I'm not leaving."

"Fine." She dropped her hand from the door frame. "I'll show you where they are."

I followed her inside. My eyes cut to the dark dining room entrance to my left then to the blinking tree pushed against the window. "Why'd you move the tree?"

Krys shrugged and waved a hand toward the hall. "They're in the bedroom. Naturally."

"You lead the way. Since you're the niece and all." I didn't trust her. And I didn't know where the nephew had gone.

She rolled her eyes and strode toward the hall.

"So, after all these years, Miss Martha Mae has a visit from her niece and a nephew." On the same day as the Forks County Savings and Loan was robbed. But I kept that part to myself. At the hall entrance, I hung back to peek into the kitchen. My eyes gravitated toward the back porch. Mrs. Boyes's star lights that had hung from the rafters now lit the floor and her trees had been knocked over. "What happened out there?"

She glanced over her shoulder. "Wind, I suppose."

"When'd you get here? I didn't see you earlier."

"Got here this morning."

"Didn't see you. Saw the nephew. Looks too old to be your brother. Where'd he go?"

"He's out," she said, skipping the family tree.

"Kind of surprising, since the roads are a sheet of black ice."

Krys shrugged and pointed to the door on the far right. "They're in there."

"Go on in," I said. "You best announce me."

"I don't think it's necessary." She reached beneath her sweater and pulled out a pistol. "Since y'all know each other so well, no introductions are needed."

Dammit. Of all the times to be right.

I lifted my hands. "You held up the bank? You and the nephew?"

"I don't believe I said any such thing." She unzipped my jacket, ran her hands down my sides, and pulled my phone from my coat pocket. "If you thought we robbed the bank, why'd you come in here? You are a stupid woman."

Also, a sick one. I hoped she picked up a good amount of germs, patting me down. She knelt, feeling inside my boots.

"You had something to do with the bank," I said. "Maybe you technically didn't rob it. Driver?"

Her eyes flicked up, giving her away.

"Left them high and dry? That's some honor among thieves. They got lucky with the weather. Otherwise, the FBI would have taken over. Now you're on the run, and you don't even have the money. You know the deputy your partners took hostage? He's mine." I gritted my teeth. "Where is he?"

"I don't know what you're talking about." She jerked to standing and motioned with the gun. "Go. Bathroom's inside."

I planted my feet, stared her in the eye. "If y'all hurt a hair on that deputy's head, I'll get you. All y'all. Every single last one."

"Kind of hard to do that now isn't it?" Her brows rose with her smirk. "I heard he barreled right in that bank, just like you did this house. Got yourself in the same predicament, didn't you?"

#HarkYouHeraldAngelAndListenUp

I RETURNED to the artist's house, fighting panic. The patrol car had parked there. They must have spoken to the police. Was an arrest made or not?

At the kitchen door, a bright spotlight blinded me. Shielding my eyes, I couldn't squint past colored lights backlit by a stark, white beam. Inside the door, rows of Christmas lights stretched across the frame. Someone had positioned a lamp just behind the door to beam through the squares of glass. The glare reminded me of professional camera lighting. Bright, stark, and hot. The artist might use something similar for her portrait painting. What was she doing beaming it at the door now?

Backing from the door, I carefully picked my way through the piles of junk and carefully stepped my way across the icy drive. More lights blared through the window and door. Old fashioned Christmas lights had been wrapped around the porch and across the entrance at knee height. Like holiday lighting for elves.

I stepped into the grass and checked my watch. It'd been a little over an hour since I'd last talked to Casey. Someone had been busy. And now I couldn't get back in the house.

Circling between the two houses, I glanced into the bedroom window. Christmas lights shone above a bed where it looked like someone slept. She didn't look well protected, not like the kitchen and front porch. An air conditioner unit stood under the window. Climbing on top, I reached to knock on the glass. Just before my knuckle rapped, I stopped. Some instinct caused me to focus on the window itself. I cocked my head, adjusted my focus, and spotted the thin wire stretched across the inside window frame.

Tripwire? For an alarm?

I hoped nothing else. As Nash often warned his more redneck clients, injury-inducing and potentially lethal booby traps were illegal. You can defend your home, but a *Home Alone* mousetrap isn't self-defense in the eyes of the law. If an intruder was hurt or died, the homeowner went to jail. And would likely get sued.

It's the threat of a lawsuit that usually makes the client change their mind about buying a security system instead of creating their own.

At the back of the house, I hopped the fence and tiptoed across the perimeter. Someone had lined the cement slab running along the side of the house with empty cans filled with coins and nails. A landmine field of noise. Christmas lights hung in tight rows in the back windows. Barricading the windows with lighting.

Their safety measures looked festive. In fact, the house had gone from Grinch cave to Whoville home in one evening.

Whether it would deter Jay or Krystal from a break-in, I wasn't sure. Maybe they'd already been arrested. It was the season of hope. Although finding "*Home Alone* meets Whoville" next door didn't give me much comfort.

Anyway, it looked like visitors weren't welcomed at the artist's house.

I jogged toward Martha Mae's house. Hoarse shouting and pounding stopped me. I listened to the rising anger. A new voice. A woman's. But the strength of her fury didn't match the strength of her voice. Hurrying toward the corner of the house, I crouched, then poked my head around the corner.

A girl — or tiny woman, hard to tell by her size and the amount of clothing she had on — pounded and kicked Martha Mae's door.

Pulling back, I leaned my head against the house and stared at the moonless sky. Now what? New people kept popping up in my simple case to retrieve a bank-robbing, cop-kidnapping granddaughter (unless she'd become a nun). I held my face in my mittened hands and sighed. My breath warmed my face for a few seconds. Dropping my hands, my skin turned damp, cold, and miserable.

Just like my day. And now, night.

The light in the Christmas tree window grew brighter. The pounding stopped. Followed by the clicks and squeaks of a door unlocking and opening.

I peeked. The tiny woman entered the house. The woman who could be Krystal had let her in.

Sucktastic. Another body for the garden hole of doom.

I had lost my Christmas hope. Where was my Hallmark Channel angel when I needed one?

19 CHERRY TUCKER

KRYS DIDN'T KNOW this wasn't my first time to be duct-taped. First time to share that experience with Pearl and my neighbor, though. Not that I enjoyed being duct-taped. In previous escapades, I'd been hogtied in various degrees by an assortment of nefarious characters. Criminals loved duct tape. And that was the sort of luck I ran. Maybe more due to my nature than luck, but that was neither here nor there.

The fact was, it took more than duct tape to get this artist down.

Not only had Pearl's ankles, wrists, and mouth been taped, she'd also been strapped to Martha Mae's toilet seat. Seeing me, Pearl's ruddy complexion had paled.

"Casey's safe," I'd said. "I know everything. The police are aware of the situation. It's all under control."

Pearl's eyes told me she knew a fibber when she saw one.

"Time for you to shut your mouth." Krys ripped off a piece of tape and slapped it over my mouth. "The police aren't aware of anything. I talked to them myself."

Lord, I thought. Jake Fells didn't know Pearl. Kind of surprising, since Pearl's mouth was bigger than mine. Why didn't Uncle

Will send an older deputy over? One who actually knew citizens? And could spot a liar?

Mrs. Boyes lay in the bathtub — also taped — with an ugly welt around her neck and another on her forehead. Her skin was pasty, and eyes closed. Unconscious. And if she didn't have a bad back now, she'd have one later, lying in a heap in a cold bathtub.

That sumbitch Santa. Strangled this sweet woman who couldn't bake worth a darn but gave out cookies and fruitcake every Christmas all the same.

I thought I might explode with anger. Heat poured off me, making my skin sticky and hair slick.

Out of places to stash bodies in the master bath, Krys forced me to sit on the sink. Threw my coat and winter accessories in a corner. She taped my wrists before taping them to the underside of the sink faucet. Pulled off my boots to tape my ankles together. Unfortunately, found the pocketknife I'd slipped in my boot, too. Ran tape back and forth over my thighs until I was attached to the single sink counter.

I'll tell you one thing, sitting in a sink basin is not comfortable in the least. But thank you, Lord, for giving me a skinny derriere despite my previous feelings on that subject.

"Try anything," said Krys, "And I'll shoot your grandma. You see the woman in the tub? That's what happens when you piss me off."

Pearl's eyes widened. She turned toward me, blinking rapidly.

I couldn't retort with the tape over my mouth, but I mentally flung a few well-chosen words at Krys. Waited until she closed the door and began working my wrists and ankles. All I needed was to jerk up and away. Or find a sharp corner to rub the tape against. However, I hadn't been taped to a faucet in my earlier duct tape experiences. Leaning back, I wiggled an elbow and succeeded in turning on the water, drenching the seat of my pants. Took another minute to knock the water off.

I was no longer hot.

Pearl snorted. Glad she still had a sense of humor. Still, I cut my eyes at her and gave her a good eye roll. She motioned with her chin at the cabinet behind me.

I scooted sideways as best I could, and after a series of misses, my right elbow bumped the bottom of the mirror. The magnet unlatched. I bent over my legs, my arms straining behind me. Leaned right and jerked up, smacking the mirror. Feeling like my arms might pull from their sockets, I flattened over my legs. The mirror swung open thirty degrees, brushing the top of my back. I nudged it farther with my right shoulder. Leaning sideways as far as possible, I pulled up behind the mirror.

I cranked my neck to see behind me. Rows of medication, ointments, powders, and lotions. I turned to see the other side. Barber scissors, nail files, manicure scissors, and other helpful items stood in a small plastic cup.

Jackpot.

I scooted back, then turned, knocking my shoulder into the shelf. Pill bottles rained over me. The plastic cup fell, spilling its contents on the sink, then rolled to the floor. Behind the open mirror, I couldn't see Pearl. I hoped she was mentally congratulating me on retrieving various cutting instruments.

Of course, I had no way of picking them up.

Round two.

I wiggled inside my wet jeans. The duct tape strap was stuck to my jeans, but I could move my thighs beneath them. Couldn't pull up my knees, though. I sucked in my stomach and backed into the faucet. Pinched my fingers. Twisted right and left. Working my fingers down the back of my pants, I pushed at the waistband. Water dripped down my back. Chills wracked my body, but I ignored them. Slowly I pulled down the jeans. Twisted and wriggled. For once the flu worked in my favor. I'd already lost weight. My jeans were loose, and my hips slipped free.

If Luke ever complained about my lack of booty, I'd use this as an example of a benefit.

Oh Lord, Luke.

The pit closed around me. Tears welled. Snot pooled in my nose. I sniffed it back.

Come on, Cherry. This is not a time to lose focus. Tuckers don't cry, we get even. Breathe. Remember Pearl and Mrs. Boyes are still here. Casey's next door with the lunatic nephew running around and the movie star PI is nowhere to be found.

My back scraped against the faucet. My fingers clawed at the denim. My shoulders hit the cabinet shelving. More bottles and tubes flew, showering the sink and floor. My hips lifted above the faucet. I had to lean back, using the cabinet to carry my weight. My thighs slid free, and a moment later, my feet climbed into the sink.

I twisted hard, trying to rip the tape on the faucet. Worked my wrists back and forth, loosening and rolling the tape. The cool air bit into my bare legs. Chills ran up my back, and sweat poured off my temples. Too intent to stop, I ignored the pain in my shoulders and arms. The rolled band of tape reached the apex of the faucet's curve and slid off in a series of jerks.

For a moment, I breathed in short puffs, then wiggled my hips through the circle of my arms. Brought them round, turned, and found the scissors. Poked them through the tape in my feet until I could rip them apart. Then scrambled out of the sink. And fell on the floor.

With my wrists still bound, I used my fingers to pull off the tape from my mouth.

Gasping, I looked up at Pearl. "How's that?"

Her eyebrows shot up, then lowered. She nodded toward her taped hands.

"I need you to hold the scissors as tight as you can, so I can rip the tape on my hands first."

Pearl shrugged.

I shoved the scissors between her fingers. She squeezed. I

pushed my duct tape binds against the blades, sawing. She dropped the scissors. We tried again.

I didn't want to worry Pearl, but my energy level was in serious trouble. If I were a video game, it'd be flashing red. The inside of my head felt like an ocean breaking on a shore. Black dots danced before my eyes. The room spun.

The scissor blade pierced the tape. I ripped my wrists apart. Dropping to all fours, I ducked my head and panted. Above me, Pearl wiggled and grunted. Tried to kick me with her taped ankles.

"Just a tic," I said. "Give me a second or I'm going to lose all the Gatorade you made me drink."

Pearl stomped her feet. I cranked my head. She was staring at the door and grunting.

Someone was in the bedroom.

My wet pants were still taped to the sink. The cabinet mirror hung open. Miss Martha Mae's toiletries and medicines littered the floor.

Pants-less, I crawled across the floor. Rose to shaky knees and locked the bathroom door. Leaned my back against the door.

"One minute," I said to Pearl. And passed out.

#DoYouHearWhatIHear #YouDon'tWantToHearWhatIHear

SOON AFTER THE TINY, angry woman entered Martha Mae's home — If the day had gone differently, I might guess her to be an overlarge elf. Her coat had a deer head silhouette painted on the back. Ornaments hung from his antlers. — Jay exited.

After trying Nash unsuccessfully, I hung up. My finger had pressed the numbers nine and one when the sound of a door closing sent shivers down my spine. After the last burst of noise, the eerie *snick* sounded foreboding. I snapped the phone shut and clutched it. From my squat against the side of the house, I peered around the corner.

Jay stood on the porch, pulling his pack of cigarettes from his coat pocket. His body faced the street, but his head moved. Scanning the neighborhood. As he looked to his right, I ducked back.

Knowing where he likely headed — exactly where I crouched — I hauled butt toward the backyard.

Oh God, I thought. I changed my mind. All I want for Christmas is peace on earth and let it begin with me.

By keeping me alive.

At the garden, I crouched behind the fence. Martha Mae's Christmas fairy lights brightened the garden, darkening the area I needed to see. And creating a nice glow on my hiding spot. I ripped the lights off the fence. Pulled them into a pile until I reached the battery box and switched them off.

Where did Jay go?

My heart pounded. Don't worry about Jay. She-Who-Could-Be-Krystal was in the house with the angry elf and the grandmothers doing who knows what.

Call 9-1-1.

I pulled the phone from my pocket. Nearby, the loud crash of breaking glass broke the stillness. The screech of an alarm jerked me out of my shocked, frozen state.

The artist's house. She had trip-wired her bedroom window. And she was sick in bed. With a pregnant sister.

Oh, my God.

Yanking the string of lights off the ground, I ran for the house. The air conditioner blocked my ability to get close to the window. The window was broken. Pieces of shattered glass covered the unit. Under the glow of the Christmas lights, a man moved around the room. Jay. He flung bedding aside. No sick artist.

Sick artist was the angry elf. But where was Casey? My stomach clenched. I glanced at my hand gripping the string of lights. Why did I bring lights? What was I going to do with this? Lasso him?

I sucked in frigid air. Held it to keep from screaming.

The overhead light blared on. Jay stood at the bedroom door. He rattled the knob, and another alarm shrieked. Leaping back, he stared at the door, then threw his body against it. A board that had been balanced above the lintel fell, raining jars and cans. Jay threw his hands over his head. Paint splashed and dripped.

Jay was a multi-colored mess. And angry.

Shiztastic. Where was Casey?

"Open this door," he shouted. "Or I'm shooting the shit out of it. The police won't get here in time, so don't bother calling them again. That was your last mistake. You and your sister's nosiness was the first. You brought this on yourself by not minding your own business. Now I'm taking care of business."

Reaching into his jacket, he pulled out a pistol.

I screamed.

Jay spun, aiming the pistol at the window.

I fell to the ground.

A shot rang out. Followed by a second blast and the sound of broken glass.

21 CHERRY TUCKER

PEARL'S MUFFLED shouting woke me up. I blinked, noted my sprawl on the bathroom floor, and crawled to standing. Feeling like a bewildered prairie dog popped from his hole, I spun between the door to Pearl. Chose the door. I pressed my ear against the crack next to the jamb. The bedroom was quiet. I scuttled back to Pearl, ripped the tape off her mouth, then used the scissors to cut her free.

"Lord, I've never been so glad that Martha Mae had one of those cushioned toilet seats." Pearl stood and stretched, rubbing her back.

Not the first words I expected.

"We need to get Mrs. Boyes out of here," I said. "And you."

"Don't forget yourself," said Pearl. "You're not fit for saving anyone. You were laid out on that floor for five minutes."

"You want me to tape you up again?" I glared at Pearl, then softened. "Sorry. Are you all right?"

"My heart is still ticking, ain't it?" She glanced at Mrs. Boyes. "Don't know if I can say the same for Martha Mae. Lord, I've been praying she'll live. They just dumped here in the bathtub, can you believe it? What kind of folks dump old ladies in bathtubs?"

"Bank robbers. I saw the nephew strangle her." I touched her cheek. "She's still alive, Pearl."

"That girl said she did it."

"Doesn't matter who did it, Mrs. Boyes needs an ambulance. You think we should lift her?" I turned to look at Pearl.

She stared at the door. "That girl has a gun, Cherry. We need to stay put until the police arrive."

"They've already been here and left again. The streets aren't good for anything but hockey. There's no rescue coming."

Her knees gave way. She plopped on the toilet seat. The cushion hissed. "I've been locked in here all this time, and the sheriff's not coming for me?"

"They didn't have probable cause to search. Krys told Deputy Fells she was you. He didn't know the difference." I swallowed. "And he was in a hurry to get back to the manhunt."

"He should have known."

"I'd told you something fishy was going on, and you didn't believe me."

"You did no such thing. And you said Santa choked his reindeer, not bank robbers strangled poor Martha Mae."

"It doesn't matter, Pearl. I'm your rescue." I placed my hands on my hips, urging my weak body to appear tough.

A tear rolled down Pearl's cheek. "Well, if that doesn't just take the cake."

"Stay in here." I felt too sorry for Pearl to be offended. "Keep the door locked. Tend to Mrs. Boyes. Jam something between the door and frame to keep Krys from opening it. If it's me, I'll say so."

"Maybe we need a secret word." Pearl sniffed. "If she can pretend to be me, that woman could pretend to be you."

"Okay." I patted Pearl's shoulder, then pulled on my boots and coat. "How about 'Merry Christmas?' I doubt a bank robber would think of such a thing."

I slowly opened the door, peering into the dark bedroom.

Sidled out and closed the door. Behind me, I heard Pearl turning the lock. I needed a weapon. I glanced at my bare legs.

Pants would also be helpful.

Dresses and blouses filled her closet. I pulled open dresser drawers, yanking out clothes until I found something that resembled sweatpants. Four sizes too big. Yanked them on, stuffed them in my boots, and tied them with a strip of material I found in a basket on the floor.

A wave of dizziness hit me hard. I sank to the floor. Heard footsteps in the hall, I slid under Mrs. Boyes's bed. Krys strode into the bedroom, eased up to the bathroom door, and listened.

For once in your life, please keep your mouth shut, Pearl.

Under the bed, dust bunnies threatened my nose. Krys wasn't moving from guard duty. I needed a distraction before she tried to open the door and find it locked. I didn't trust Pearl to stay quiet, the lock to hold, or Krys to not use her gun as a door opener.

I backed out from under the bed on the other side and crawled into the hallway. Tiptoed into the kitchen. Set the microwave to thirty seconds. Took ten seconds considering a heavy fruitcake versus Martha Mae's block of knives. I'd have a better chance of taking out Krys with a fruitcake lob to the head than using a knife in a gunfight. For safekeeping, I tossed the knife block into the garbage.

Twenty seconds. Dancing at the countdown, I looked left toward the garage door where I knew Martha Mae would have wicked gardening tools. Mrs. Boyes was a gardener. Kept me in tomatoes all summer. Glanced right and saw a shovel among all the debris on the screened-in porch.

Looked wicked enough to me. And with a longer reach than a carving knife. Less risky than a fruitcake.

The clock flashed ten. I scooted toward the porch, lugged open the sliding door, and hopped into the frigid night air. Grabbed the shovel. Scurried into the living room. Snatched the

TV remote off the coffee table. Flattened against the wall next to the hall entrance.

The microwave beeped long and strong. Three times.

I gulped air. Three times.

A moment later, I heard Krys pattering down the hall. At her "What the hell," I smacked the TV remote, raised the volume, and tossed it. Gripped the shovel and swung it over my shoulder.

Across the living room, in matching blue headbands and rolled pants, Bing Crosby and Danny Kaye sang "Sisters."

Krys's "What the hell" rang out again. Footsteps rang in the kitchen.

My stomach tossed and churned. I tightened my grip and prayed for good aim. Also, not to vomit.

A boot and the muzzle of her pistol appeared first. Taking a deep breath, I waited until she stepped into the room. Swung.

And a shot cracked the air just as Bing slapped Danny with his fan.

#HardCandyChristmas

CLUTCHING MY HEART, I huddled on the ground next to the air conditioner unit. Across from me, Martha Mae's window had cracked, splintering into what looked like a giant snowflake. A center the size of a bullet hole. I looked up. Something blocked the artist's window. Rising slowly, I kept my back to the house and peeked. Jay stood with his back to the window. Pushed up against the broken frame.

What had happened? I'd heard two shots. Jay had aimed at me.

My legs shook. I blinked past the spots dancing before my eyes. Okay, don't think about Jay's gun. Think about the second shot. Because it hadn't sounded like the first. Muffled. But louder.

"I know where you're standing," yelled a voice from inside. "I've had tactical training and I ain't shooting with birdshot. These slugs will go through more than one wall. You think this hole is big? Think about what it'll do to a body. Get out of my house. Same way you came in."

Casey. Holy shizolis. The pregnant sister had blown a hole through the drywall with her sister's shotgun.

I had to stop the gun battle before someone was shot for real. A wall might slow a bullet, but it would still penetrate. She and her baby were at risk.

"Do it now," urged my inner Julia Pinkerton. "Save the woman and child while you still have the element of surprise. Her shotgun blast has him stunned. He's ready to climb out the window. In a second, he'll turn around."

All I had was a string of Christmas lights. I patted my pockets. And a candy cane.

Craptastic.

But if I wasn't so afraid of hurting someone, I'd be better armed.

One end of the candy cane had been sucked to a sharp point. Yanking off my mittens, I tested it against my thumb. No blood, but it made a small hole just the same. My (ruined) puffy jacket had kept it safe.

Time was of the essence, as they say. Julia Pinkerton had once stopped a would-be kidnapper with a homemade shiv made from a lipstick tube and a re-molded Jolly Rancher.

Not the time to remember Julia Pinkerton wasn't real. Or that the writers were sometimes lazy.

I sprung to my feet. Gripped the taped end of the candy cane in my fist. Flung the string of lights like a scarf around my neck. Climbed on the air conditioner, kicking off glass.

Grasping Jay's paint-covered collar with my left hand, I jabbed the pointed end of the candy cane into the side of his neck. Sliced across his skin. Then pressed the point in the softer flesh in the hollow of his jaw, beneath his ear.

Jay cursed. A jagged string of red dots crossed his neck. He clamped a hand over mine, letting go at the sound of the pump of the shotgun's slide.

"Hold it there, bucko," said Casey. "I see you through the hole. That first shot was a warning. I've got your chest sighted."

"I wouldn't move." Using my low, menacing Julia Pinkerton-on-the-prowl voice, I repeated the line from *Julia Pinkerton: Teen Detective* Season Eight, Episode Two. "Not unless you want to lose your carotid artery to my *sweet* blade."

I pressed harder, puncturing the skin. Hoped he didn't notice the peppermint scent. "Only takes two minutes to bleed out. Now, drop your weapon. Hands in the air."

"I'm going to kill you," said Jay. "Then I'm going to kill her."

"Casey, I've got Jay by the throat. But don't let that stop you." I studied the hardening rainbow colors on his hair and clothes. Drywall dust blew through the air. "I don't think you want to mess with these girls, Jay. They take home defense seriously."

"Drop your weapon, jackass," said Casey. "I've got the safety off. Maizie, y'all get out of the way. This shot will blow through him."

Jay cursed. A thunk sounded near his feet.

"He's unarmed, Maizie," yelled Casey. "I'm still covering you."

"Hands behind your back, Jay," I said. "Casey, if he tries anything, shoot first. I'm tying him up."

"This is not over," said Jay.

"Sit on the ledge," I growled.

White-knuckled with cold, I gripped the candy cane, matching the speed of my squat to Jay's sit. With my left hand, I yanked on the lights, pulling them off my neck. "Hands together. Cover me, Casey."

He strung an interesting litany of obscenities together.

Pocketing the candy cane, I blew on my hands and flexed my numb fingers. I wrapped the wired lighting around his wrists, yanked the wrists together, and wrapped them again. Pulling the string tight against his body, I wrapped his wrists to his torso. "If you move too much, the glass bulbs will break and cut your skin."

"I hope it cuts him up good," said Casey. "I'm coming in the bedroom."

In the distance, I heard a truck's rumble.

"Casey," I hollered. "Someone's coming. Maybe the police."

The bedroom door banged open. "Man, Cherry stuck that doorstop in tight. What a mess. Paint and glass everywhere." Casey stomped into the bedroom, swinging the shotgun before her. "That's Nik. I called him a while ago. As a Slavic, he knows how to drive on ice. And he's got friends with a salt truck. Don't know how they got one, but they do. It's better not to know."

"You meet any Russians in prison, Jay?" I asked. "Her husband's Russian."

"Russian-ish. So are his friends." She aimed the gun barrel at Jay. "They don't play around. You better hope the police come before they learn you were going to shoot me."

"You got this, Casey?" I was a little worried about leaving Jay alone with her. For Jay's sake. Casey had the ferocious look of a mother bear protecting her cub. "I need to get to Martha Mae's. Find out what's going on over there."

"Yes, ma'am. You want his gun?" She'd squatted to scoop up the pistol and used the bed to climb back to her feet.

"Krystal had nothing to do with this," Jay spoke quickly, startling me. "It was all me."

"Are you confessing?" I pulled my phone from my pocket. "I want this recorded."

"Yep, I did it all. Krystal was just visiting her aunt."

Over Jay's head, I locked eyes with Casey. She shrugged. Leaned against the nightstand. Repositioned the gun.

"What exactly did you do?" I said. "For the record?"

"Drove the getaway car for the bank robbery. I can name everyone involved. Give a guess as to where they went after they split."

"You know where they took the cop?" said Casey sharply.

He hesitated. "No."

Casey pumped the shotgun's slide.

"I can give you all that information if you let Krystal go. She had nothing to do with this," said Jay. "I've done time. I know when I've lost. I'm willing to go back. Just let her go."

"What about Martha Mae Boyes? And Pearl?" I said. "What happened to them?"

"They're next door. I take full responsibility. Had them captive in the bathroom."

"You sumbitch," said Casey.

"I wasn't going to kill them. Just holding them until Krystal could get out of here. Same with you. We just needed to get gone first."

I looked at Casey. The police would want this information, but I didn't trust Jay. Why would he give up so easily? We might have double-teamed him, but he'd flipped from maniacal to melancholy.

Which reminded me of an episode of *Kung Fu Kate*, "Double-Crossed Deuces." I'd done that show at twelve, but still. The antagonist had been covering for someone. Like Jay might be doing for Krystal. But he must know, Krystal would still be considered an accomplice.

"You're her father," I said. "You think you're helping Krystal."

His body tensed.

"Looks like she's past helping." Casey had picked up a pad of paper from the nightstand and flipped through the pages. "My sister drew everything she saw today. First picture shows Santa choking Mrs. Boyes. Except Santa's beard and hat had come off. It's a woman."

"That don't mean nothing," said Jay.

"You might not know this, but my sister is famous in these parts for her ability to quick sketch accurately. My uncle's hired her to sketch profiles at the sheriff's department. And she's worked at Six Flags all during high school."

"What else is in that sketchbook?" I said. "That's evidence."

"You." Casey smirked. Tossing the sketchbook on the bed, she cradled the shotgun. "And this man showing me, you, and then Pearl the inside of Mrs. Boyes's house."

Oh boy, evidence of my breaking and entering. Oh well. There were more important considerations now.

"Do you have a phone on you, Jay?" I said. "Will Krystal answer if you call?"

At his nod, I reached into his coat pocket and retrieved the phone. He walked me through dialing Krystal's number.

"Well?" said Casey.

"She's not answering." I pocketed his phone.

"Dammit," said Jay. "Tell her I've given myself up. Immediately. Before you say anything else. Have her call me. I'll tell her. Before she does something she regrets."

"Casey, don't shoot him unless you absolutely have to. I'm going next door." I hopped off the air conditioner.

Then froze at the sound of a gunshot.

I whirled around, searching the artist's bedroom. But the sound hadn't come from this house. Casey had jumped to her feet and repositioned the shotgun. Jay had twisted to look out the window.

I leaned over the air conditioner. "Casey, can you get him into another room?"

She nodded.

"It's too late," said Jay morosely. "Damn girl."

"What's too late?" Scenes from every horror movie I'd ever known crossed my mind.

"Krystal crossed the line. There's no getting her back now."

"What are you talking about?"

"It's my fault. I couldn't protect Krystal when I was doing time. She managed to stay away from the law this long. Krystal's smart. But I told her to keep away from that woman, she'd lead her down the wrong road. Krys thinks she can play people, but I know better. That woman can talk her way in and out of situations better than Krys."

"What woman?" Please don't say, Celia Fowler, I thought. Please, don't let it be the grandma.

"Don't matter now," said Jay. "I tried to help her out of this situation. Willing to lay my life down for that girl. Go back to prison for my baby. But apples don't fall far from trees."

"Keep him talking, Casey. I've got to go next door to help." I glanced at Casey over his shoulder.

Her shoulders shook, but her dark eyes had shrunk into two slits, narrowed with rage. "We need to know what's going on to help the police when they come."

"I heard that shot, same as you," she said. "And my sister doesn't have a gun. I know what's going on. You're going to get yourself killed, too."

"We don't know what happened." But as I ran, I prayed for to my Hallmark Channel angel. Please, please don't let anyone die.

#GeeIWishIWereBackInTheArmy

NASH HADN'T TRAINED me in tactical defense situations. Despite what you see in the movies, private investigators aren't involved in shootouts. Nash hadn't bothered to train me much on anything. Except how to answer his phone, use his billing software, and to jiggle the office toilet handle when the water doesn't stop running.

Although I often discredited the writers on *Julia Pinkerton* and *Kung Fu Kate* for their unbelievable plots, my multitude of directors (TV production is a career meat grinder) had excelled at coaching me into making the unbelievable look believable. With the help of experts. Namely Detective Earl King, who showed me how to hold a gun properly and the real way officers clear a room.

Which was how I approached Martha Mae's house. Checking corners before proceeding. Running the wall. Scanning windows from the side. I carefully climbed over the ice-coated porch rail and sidled to the front window. Repositioned to look again. Got a look from another angle. Hesitated. Then rang the doorbell and knocked.

An older woman in a sweatshirt decorated with goats answered. "Cherry told me not to let anyone in, but I figure if you're coming to kill us, you won't bother to ring the bell."

"Are you Pearl?" I said. "Are you all right?"

"My sciatica is acting up, thanks to sitting on a toilet all day, but other than that I'm fine." She stepped back, studying me. "You must be the nosy movie star."

"I'm Maizie Albright. Not a movie star, although I've done plenty of TV movies." I automatically stuck my hand out to shake hers. Luckily, I was used to improv. My adrenaline kick had subsided into a low hum and I turned myself over to another kind of instinct. Small talk with fans. "Now I'm a private investigator. Or at least training to be one. I hope. If it works out. Anyway, here to help."

"Can't say we need your help now unless you're driving an ambulance or a paddy wagon. Do you know where that man went?"

"Jay's been apprehended. Casey's got the shotgun on him. And help is on its way. I think."

She snorted. "Hope that baby doesn't throw her off balance. Guess you ought to come in. Colder than an Eskimo's outhouse out here."

I followed her inside. On the floor, a woman lay hogtied with what looked like lengths of fabric. She ducked her head up to study me.

"Are you Krystal Fowler?"

"Go to hell."

"Told us her name was Krys. I'm guessing her last name isn't Kringle." Pearl trotted to the couch, sat, and reached for the coffee cup on the coffee table.

White Christmas played on the TV. If it weren't for the hamstrung prisoner on the floor, it'd be a cozy scene.

"I'm watching her. I've got her gun right here. Shot it up the fireplace flue to show her I knew what I was doing." Pearl patted the pistol next to her thigh. "I didn't want to shoot up Martha Mae's house. It's a mess as it is."

"I'm going to kill you, old woman," said Krystal.

"You and what army? Try it, and I'll shoot you plain as day. I raise goats. I'm tougher than I look." Pearl's attention swiveled to the TV. She patted her chest and sniffled. "That Bing Crosby. Gets me every time."

Krystal's head thunked to the ground.

I'd entered a Christmas episode of *The Twilight Zone*.

"Aren't you worried she'll escape?" I said.

"Nah," said Pearl. "Too many knots. Plus, I have no compunction shooting someone who'd tied me to a toilet for hours on end. I'm stiffer than a corpse."

Okay, then. Take a note not to mess with Pearl.

"Where's Martha Mae Boyes?" I asked.

"On the bed. Took some work to get her there. She came to for a minute, but she's laid flat. That's why we need the ambulance. That girl choked her. I'm surprised Martha Mae didn't have a heart attack, but she's like me. Tough old bird."

"The artist?"

"Cherry? Passed out on the bedroom floor." Pearl shook her head, looking disgusted. "That's what happens when you overexert yourself with the flu. I warned her."

"Maybe you should check on them? I'll watch Krystal while you do."

"All right. I could use a break." Pearl rose, rubbing her lower back. She pointed toward the TV. "They're going to do that modern dance scene, anyway. Never cared for that number."

I waited until I heard the bedroom door close, then squatted next to their prisoner. "Krystal, what happened to the police officer? The one you took hostage?"

Her head flopped to the other side, facing the tree. "Probably dead."

My stomach lurched. "But where is he?"

She laughed. "Doesn't matter now."

Glancing up, I spotted the shovel leaning against the wall. Oh my God. The garden hole.

"Pearl, I've gotta go back out," I yelled. "Call for another ambulance."

24 CHERRY TUCKER

I WOKE WITH A START, finding myself on the floor of a dark room. Leaping up, I lost my pants, tripped, and hit the floor again. I'd forgotten I had used my homemade belt to bind Krys's hands. After I repeatedly screamed "Merry Christmas" for what felt like forever, Pearl had bounded from the bathroom. I sent her to search for rope. Pearl brought me quilting strips and binding tape. Not my first choice in trussing material. But what was I going to do? Use a string of Christmas lights?

Snatching another strip of cloth from Martha Mae's basket, I tied the sweatpants around my waist and crept down the hall. *White Christmas* still played on the TV in the living room. I took it as a good sign and entered. Sighed with relief to see our prisoner still captive.

Pearl waved the gun.

I leaned over her. "Still unconscious? I walloped her pretty good."

"Naw," said Pearl. "Asleep. Told me my movie was boring."

"What kind of criminal falls asleep on the living room floor?"

"It's been a long day." Pearl patted the couch next to her. "Come watch *White Christmas* with me. You just missed that movie star gal. She was here earlier, then ran out. Came back unbelievably dirty."

"Why?"

"Dug up Martha Mae's garden. Strange night all around. But she was real excited about something she thinks is in the garage. Spied on those two earlier and overheard them talking in there. The movie star thought something important was in the trunk. She's gone back to get the keys from Martha Mae's nephew. She and Casey's got him tied up over at the house."

"He's not Mrs. Boyes's nephew," I said. "He's a bank robber. And he strangled Martha."

"The movie star said he didn't strangle Martha Mae."

"What does she know?"

"It's you who knows. You drew the girl strangling Martha Mae." Pearl pointed to a garbage bag under the tree. "And look in there. But don't touch it. It's evidence. Or so says Movie Star. She was all tore up about this gal being the one to strangle Martha and rob a bank. I think she hoped that man had done it all."

"Who wouldn't be tore up, but why does she care who did it?"

"Said it was the grandma's fault, but I didn't see any grandma threatening to kill us, did you?"

I shook my head. Maybe it was the flu. Maybe it was Pearl. But her explanation lacked something. Namely reason and logic. Hurrying over to the tree, I snatched an icicle ornament and used it to open the muddy bag and draw out the clothing inside.

"A Santa suit," I said.

"For a girl," said Pearl. "That nephew is too big. It's Krys's suit. You saw Krys strangling Martha Mae. The nephew is her father. He's a piece of work, mind you. But he didn't instigate any of this. He arrived to clean up the mess."

"Clean up the mess by terrorizing us." I pushed the Santa suit back in the bag.

"Oh, not just terrorize. The movie star said he meant to kill us. Get rid of the evidence, so Krys here wouldn't get caught. 'Course he probably meant to split her share of the bank's money. He's a felon, too."

"A felon for a father."

"And bank robber for a grandfather, or so said the movie star. You can't pick your relatives." Pearl shook her head. "Speaking of relatives, your sister blew a hole in your bedroom wall."

"Did anybody think to call the sheriff about all this?"

"Of course, we did. Who do you think we are?"

Obviously not suffering from victim PTSD. Or maybe that came later. Right now, Pearl looked ready for chestnuts roasting over an open fire. Humming along to the movie.

"Casey said Nik called his foreign friends," said Pearl. "They're bringing a salt truck. You ever heard of such a thing?"

"I don't want to know how they got a hold of a salt truck, but we need it. Uncle Will can get here faster. Toss them in the—" I almost bit my tongue in my haste to change subjects. "Krys drove the getaway car. But Deputy Fells said the driver left when the bank's alarm went off. The bank robbers were given a van, but they never found Luke in the van or at the Winn Dixie."

Shaking her head, Pearl compressed her lips into a grim line.

"She could have been waiting to meet them." I leaned over Krys. "We searched her for weapons, but did we get her keys?"

"I told you that movie star went to get the man's keys. But the stuff from her pockets is on the kitchen table."

"If Movie Star is right, they must have driven separately." I ran toward the kitchen and saw the keys in a pile with a phone, lighter, and a small plastic ammo box. Holding my sweatpants in one hand, I grabbed the keys and darted through the door to the garage. Two vehicles. I pressed the key's unlock button.

One car flashed its lights.

I banged on the garage door opener to light the room and ran to the Toyota's trunk. Behind me, the door rumbled and lifted. I popped the trunk release and lifted the lid.

Tears welled in my eyes. Luke lay curled in the trunk, his

head bent and limbs coiled to fit the space. He'd been gagged and bound with zip-ties. Stripped of his coat, boots, and gear. A nasty cut marked his forehead. One eye had purpled. A bloody gash behind his ear revealed his takedown. Blue veins stood stark against his normally sun-browned skin, now turned white with cold.

They'd turned my tough, rugged officer into a human popsicle.

Anger stoked my fever. Tears blurred my eyes. I clawed my way toward the top of the pit, scrabbling against the long dark tunnel, and a howling sob tore from my chest.

"You've been here the entire time. Why didn't they tell me what had happened to you? I would have kicked doors down to get to you." I reached to stroke a dusky curl off his forehead, then shrugged out of my coat to lay it over him. "You're so cold."

One gray eye opened slowly and blinked. He groaned through the gag. His big body trembled and shuddered, trying to fight the binds.

"Let me find something to cut you out of there." I scurried through the garage and returned with pruning clippers. A minute later, I helped him to uncurl, cringing at his sluggish, stiff movements. I climbed into the trunk to pull his trembling body against mine. I wanted to hurry him into the house, but Luke could barely move.

"Lord, you're colder than death. We need to get you in a bath or something."

"You're so warm. Scorching." He pressed against me, snuggling me into arms. "I can think of a better way to heat up than a bath."

I pulled back. "Really? You've been stuck in a trunk for who knows how long. You probably have frostbite and a concussion. That's the first thing you think of?"

"I'll admit if I were leaning against the sheriff, that wouldn't be my first thought." He smiled weakly, but his eyes told a different story. "Where's Sheriff Thompson? Why isn't he here? Where am I? Did the team apprehend the bank heist gang?"

"I'm your rescuer. You are next door to my house. Long story. Your team consists of me, Pearl, Casey, and some movie star private detective."

"What?" He swayed.

I caught him before he tried to climb out of the trunk.

"The sheriff never should've let them go. Those bastards pistol-whipped me. I woke up in here, then couldn't stay awake in the cold. Tried to knock out the back lights, but I couldn't move. Felt like a human pretzel."

"Uncle Will knew they'd kill you otherwise." I pulled him against me. "It's not your fault."

"It shouldn't have happened." He fell silent, tensing against another onslaught of shaking. "Damn, I hate how weak I feel."

"Tell me about it. I've been saying that all day."

"In a minute. You have the flu. You should be in bed." He pulled my forehead to his lips. "Are you hot with fever or am I that cold? This isn't making sense. How did you end up here? Where is everyone?"

"Later." I caught him against my shoulder, feeling another tremor tear through him. "Right now, we're getting you in the house. Pearl's inside. She'll fix you up."

"Just a minute." He slipped his arms around me, pulling me against his chest.

Through his shirt, his chilled flesh cooled my hot cheek. I wrapped my arms around him, and his taut muscles shivered at my touch. My sister used to say we were like fire and ice. Tonight, it was a literal interpretation.

Luke rubbed his cheek against my hair. "Cherry, lying in that trunk, I thought I was going to die from exposure. I kept thinking about what it would do to you. I know how this time of year makes you feel." His chest rose and released slowly. "I'm sorry. I offered to be the hostage exchange. It's my job. I knew the risks. But…"

He swallowed hard. "Your Christmas was ruined. Again. Forgive me?"

I didn't want him to see my tears, but I drew away from his chest anyway. Placed my warm hands against his cold cheeks. And stared into his somber gray eyes.

"I don't know what you're talking about. I couldn't have asked for a better Christmas." I leaned in, using a kiss to heat his frosty lips. "Best Christmas ever."

#AllIWantForChristmas #IsASaltTruck #AndYou

THE CAVALRY ARRIVED in the guise of five large men with Eastern European accents. The smallest one — only six feet — ran up the porch steps, tripped over the lighting, and smacked his head on the wooden porch floor. The other four followed him inside the house, laughing and taking turns at head-splat sounds.

The banter stopped at the site of our prisoner.

While Nik dropped to his knees to press his face against his wife's belly, the others surrounded Jay, cracking their knuckles and uttering low, threatening phrases in a foreign language.

"He should be in police custody," I reminded them. "Anything that happens to him now is not self-defense. You could go to jail."

They ignored me.

"Or be sued."

Grumbling, they grabbed chairs from the kitchen. Circling

Jay with their chairs, they continued the foreign threats. But half-heartedly. And while checking their phones.

"It's Pearl. Sheriff Thompson's on his way over," said Casey, one ear on the phone and a hand around her husband's waist. "Now that y'all are here, he wants you to drive that truck around town, so his deputies don't wreck their cars. He wants a clear path for the patrol cars and ambulances coming for Mrs. Boyes and Luke."

"How is the deputy?" I asked.

She hooted. "Sounds like Cherry's defrosting Luke."

"Smart man," said Nik.

"Not really. Luke's going to end up with the flu," said Casey. "And then we'll have two eating chicken soup instead of turkey on Christmas day."

"Turkey." Nik made a face. "We should have goose."

"Whoever heard of goose for Christmas dinner? I'm going to make hot chocolate for everyone," said Casey. "But first I gotta tee-tee. This baby's dancing on my bladder like she's at a house party. Someone put those lights back on the tree. Cherry's got them strung up in the windows. I guess she was hoping to electrocute the bank robbers."

"He," said Nik. "It is boy. First born in my family is always the boys."

"Sorry to disappoint you, but I could tell by the way I held Daddy's shotgun that we're having a girl." Casey stuck her hands on her hips. "The girls in our family have excellent aim. Cody and Grandpa can't hit the side of a barn."

The Hallmark Channel always used "quirky" to describe small-town characters. Maybe "dangerous" was more appropriate.

The doorbell rang. The Russian-ish salt truck gang looked up from their phones.

"Police," I cried. "Finally."

"Not yet." Nik dropped his hands from Casey's hips. "A truck followed us from highway. It stopped next door. Let me check."

I moved behind him. "I've got a candy cane shiv if you need it."

Nik looked through the peephole, then cracked the door. "What you want?"

"Is Maizie Albright in there?"

Nash.

I clapped my hands, closed my eyes, and thanked my Hallmark Channel angel. "I'm here, Nash. Let him in."

Nik stepped aside, and Wyatt Nash walked through the door. His tall, strapping physique matched those of the salt truck gang, but before a round of alpha chest-beating began, he gave the group a deferential nod. His light blue eyes swept the room, noted Jay on the floor—still tied in Christmas lights—then rested on me. Placing a hand on my shoulder, he squeezed, then patted awkwardly.

This is what happens when you deny your feelings. Awkward patting.

As for me, I grinned like an idiot, indulging in the slight touch of the awkward pat.

"You look…like you've had a long day," said Nash. "I wish I'd been here to help."

I smiled, knowing my clothes and face were mud-splattered, paint stained my hands, and my chapped skin had turned red. But at least I smelled like candy canes.

After quick introductions and an even quicker assessment of the situation, he glanced at me. "Miss Albright, we need to talk."

"Y'all can use the guest bedroom for privacy," said Casey. "Mind the mess from the shotgun blast."

Nash's eyebrows lifted. Without remarking, he followed me to the bedroom. Seeing the blast hole, he crossed the room, examined the gash, then set an eyeball to it. Rising, he turned toward me. "Did you have anything to do with this hole?"

"That was Casey. The pregnant sister. She shot through the wall. But Jay shot at me first."

He took two steps to cross the room. Grabbing my shoulders,

he lifted me slightly. Catching himself, he dropped his hands. "Maizie. Miss Albright."

"He was going to shoot Casey. I had to do something."

"And what did you do?" His cool blue eyes burned through me.

"Stabbed him with a candy cane and tied him up."

"With tree lights?"

"It was all I had."

"The police."

"Came, left, and did nothing."

"They had their hands full."

"We had bank robbers, too. And to think, Krystal's grandma is the one who sent us here." I chewed my thumbnail, fighting tears again. "Nash, Jay blames Mrs. Fowler for Krystal's crimes. Krystal drove the getaway car and willingly left a deputy to freeze to death in her trunk. Attacked her great aunt to use her home for a safe house. Then tied up her, an elderly woman, and the neighbor girl sick with the flu, and left them in Martha Mae's bathroom."

"Are you sure it was Krystal and not Jim Riley who did all that?"

"He's not much better. Planned on helping her to get rid of the evidence. I don't think he wanted to kill anyone, but he would have to protect his daughter."

"Jim Riley specifically said Mrs. Fowler directed this?"

"He said he told Krystal to 'stay away from her.' And said she could talk her way in and out of situations better than Krystal. What kind of grandma encourages behavior like bank robbing?"

"Mrs. Fowler checks out. Krystal's mother, however, did not. There's good reason to believe she's one of the culprits who robbed the bank. Evidently, they split up after the sheriff arranged their escape. I hope they caught them."

"Not the grandmother?" I swallowed hard. "Celia's a good grandma? Her house was full of unwrapped products. I thought they were stolen."

"Just a home shopping nut." Nash grinned. "She'll probably want to bake you cookies. Once she gets over the fact that her granddaughter's a felon."

I squeezed my eyes shut, imagining myself bringing Christmas cookies to Mrs. Fowler. Cookies and gumdrops. Remi would like her, too. She could tell us stories about her bank-robbing husband and con-artist daughter and grand-daughter.

Maybe I shouldn't share my adopted grandmother with Remi. She had Carol Lynn's mother, after all.

"You were right," I sighed. "Krystal wasn't a nun. I hoped she'd turn out differently. I didn't get Mrs. Fowler's grand-daughter back to her."

"Aw, kid." Nash let out a big breath. "I don't like that about myself. It's better that you see the good in people first before you suspect the bad. By the way, you did find the granddaughter. And saved several grandmothers from her in the process."

"I kept trying to call you." Tears welled. I pinched the skin on my thumb, knowing good investigators don't cry. Particularly when they're no longer in danger. Except for my toes. Still numb. They were going to take a while to recover. "You said you'd always answer."

"I'm sorry, kid. Bad reception. I drove through the storm. But I'm here." He held out his arms and dropped them. Again. "I told you to just watch the house. Go to a motel."

"I couldn't." I sniffled. "Not knowing these people were in danger."

"That's why I had to come. And got here too late." He rubbed his jaw. Paced a small circle three times. Then stopped in front of me. "Dammit. Come here, Maizie."

I fell into his arms. Pressed my head against his shoulder. The leather felt cold and hard. Unzipped his bomber jacket and burrowed against his warm, firm chest. And cried.

Nash stroked my back. Ran his hands through my hair. Then caught my chin in his palm. Gently, he raised my face, meeting my gaze with his. "Please don't cry, Maizie. You're safe. They're safe. That's all that matters."

"Also, I'm finally warm," I whispered. "Thank you."

"Merry Christmas." Nash kissed the tip of my nose. "Let's get you home to Remi. In the morning, we'll follow the salt truck trail home. You've done enough here."

"Nash," I spoke drowsily. "What did you want to do tomorrow? On Christmas Eve?"

"This." Cupping my face between his two large palms, he brushed his lips against mine. "Merry Christmas, Maizie."

Christmas wishes do come true. Thank you, Hallmark Channel angels.

The End.

THANK YOU READERS

On A VIEW TO A CHILL

Writing a mystery from two points of view with two protagonists was a challenge I enjoyed. I like "upping the ante" when it comes to writing and this *Rashomon* approach gave me the kind of creative test I relish. I hope you enjoyed it as much as I did writing it!

If you haven't read Cherry Tucker previously, this book lands somewhere after book six. For Maizie, it's more vague, but let's call it 2.5. :)

This tale was originally written for an anthology I did with twelve other cozy mystery writers, THE 12 SLAYS OF CHRISTMAS. The anthology was enormously successful and made the Wall Street Journal's bestselling ebook list December 14, 2017. But even better, the anthology was created to raise money for pets displaced in Hurricanes Harvey, Irma, and Maria. We raised a lot of money for local pet rescue organizations in Texas and Florida, plus gave money to the ASPCA.

Read on to learn more about Maizie Albright Star Detective and the Cherry Tucker Mystery series.

If you enjoyed this story, go to my website at

LarissaReinhart.com and join my VIP Readers group. You'll be the first to learn of my new releases, my upcoming projects, and exclusive giveaways including bonus content, monthly drawings, free downloads, and signed book giveaways at each new release.

You'll also receive a short story gift as a thank you for subscribing, PIG'N A POKE, the prequel to THE CUPID CAPER. I love my readers!

Thank you!

Larissa

LARISSA'S GIFT FOR YOU

PIG'N A POKE
A Finley Goodhart Crime Caper prequel
When a winter storm traps ex-con Finley at the Pig'N a Poke
roadhouse, she finds her criminal past useful in solving a
murder.
Free for my VIP Readers!

Keep up with Larissa's latest releases, sales, and events (plus
monthly giveaways, release drawings, and exclusive downloads)
by joining her monthly readers' email group — https://www.
larissareinhart.com/larissasreaders — and receive *Pig'N A Poke*
as a gift.

You'll also receive other bonus content that's exclusive for her
VIP Readers like series order guides, deleted scenes, and book
related recipes.

Note: Larissa will not share your email address and you can
unsubscribe at any time.

MEET MAIZIE ALBRIGHT

"A RAUCOUS AND ADDICTING READ"

"Child star and hilarious hot mess Maizie Albright trades
Hollywood for the backwoods of Georgia and pure delight
ensues. Maizie's my new favorite escape from reality."

GRETCHEN ARCHER, USA TODAY BESTSELLING
AUTHOR OF THE DAVIS WAY CRIME CAPER SERIES

For fans of romantic comedy mysteries like Meg Cabot's SIZE 12 IS NOT FAT and Stephanie Bond's BODY MOVERS, *The Wall Street Journal* bestselling author, Larissa Reinhart, brings her fans the first in the Maizie Albright Star Detective series, *Hot Mystery Reviews'* **"Top 10 Mysteries for Book Clubs."**

Three Teen Choice Awards, One Emmy Nomination, and several Maxim covers later, Maizie Albright was an ex-teen star, stuck in reality show hell, and standing before a California judge.
She has one chance for a new life: return home to Black Pine, Georgia, and get a job that has nothing to do with show business.
So why not become a private detective—the person she played during the happiest days of her life?
Maybe because...
First: She's got 10 days to get and keep the job.
Second: She has to convince the only private investigator in town to hire her.
Third: She lost the client's wife on the first day. (And the woman may be dead...)
Fourth: She just might be falling in love with her new boss. And she just might have lost him his business.
But what has she got to lose, other than imprisonment, her dignity, and possibly, her life?

"Maizie Albright is the kind of fresh, fun, and feisty star detective' I love spending time with, a kind of Nancy Drew meets Lucy Ricardo. Move over, Janet Evanovich. Reinhart is my new 'star mystery writer!'" — Penny Warner, Author of Death of a Chocolate Cheater and The Code Busters Club

"Sassy, sexy, and fun, 15 Minutes is hours of enjoyment—and a wonderful start to a fun new series from the charmingly Southern-fried Reinhart."— Phoebe Fox, author of The Breakup Doctor series

"**Armed with humor, charm, and stubborn determination, Maizie is a breath of fresh air**. I adored every second of 15 Minutes."— Terri L. Austin, bestselling author of the Rose Strickland Mysteries and the Null for Hire series.

"Larissa writes a delightful book. Suspense, romance, and some funny situations. **Maizie's a teen star grown up to new possibilities**." — Sharon Salituro, Fresh Fiction

"**This new series is a great mix of Hollywood with Southern charm**. This story is totally unpredictable with lots of twists and turns. Can't wait to see what the future holds for Maizie!" — Book Babble

Books in the Maizie Albright Star Detective series:
- **15 MINUTES**
- **16 MILLIMETERS**
- **A VIEW TO A CHILL**
- **NC-17**
- **18 CALIBER** (2020)

MEET CHERRY TUCKER

"LAUGH-OUT-LOUD FUNNY AND AS SOUTHERN AS SWEET TEA AND CHEESE GRITS"

"Reinhart is a truly talented author and this book was one of the best cozy mysteries we reviewed this year. We highly recommend this book to all lovers of mystery books."

– MYSTERY TRIBUNE

From *Wall Street Journal* bestselling author, Larissa Reinhart. The first in the sassy and Southern Cherry Tucker cozy mystery series, a *Woman's World Magazine* 2018 book club pick, Daphne Du Maurier finalist, The Emily finalist, Dixie Kane Memorial Winner, and Night Owl Review top pick.

In Halo, Georgia, folks know Cherry Tucker as big in mouth, small in stature, and able to sketch a portrait faster than buckshot rips from a ten gauge — but commissions are scarce. So when the well-heeled Branson family wants to memorialize their murdered son in a coffin portrait, Cherry scrambles to win their patronage from her small town rival.

As the clock ticks toward the deadline, Cherry faces more trouble than just a controversial subject. Between ex-boyfriends, her flaky family, an illegal gambling ring, and outwitting a killer on a spree, Cherry finds herself painted into a corner she'll be lucky to survive.

"**An entertaining mystery full of quirky characters and solid plotting**...Highly recommended for anyone who likes their mysteries strong and their mint juleps stronger!" – Jennie Bentley, *New York Times* Bestselling Author of *Flipped Out*

"The tone of this marvelously cracked book is not unlike Sophie Littlefield's brilliant *A Bad Day for Sorry*, as author Reinhart dishes out shovelfuls of ribald humor and mayhem. **It takes a rare talent to successfully portray a beer-and-hormone-addled artist as a sympathetic and worthy heroine, but Reinhart pulls it off with tongue-in-cheek panache.**" – *Mystery Scene Magazine*

"Don't miss Portrait of a Dead Guy by Larissa Reinhart! **Portrait is pure enjoyment, a laugh out loud mystery with some Southern romance thrown in. Five stars.**" — Lynn Farris, National Mystery Review Examiner at Examiner.com

"**Laugh-out-loud funny and as Southern as sweet tea and cheese grits**, Larissa Reinhart's masterfully crafted whodunit, Portrait of a Dead Guy, provides high-octane action with quirky, down-home characters and a trouble-magnet heroine who'll steal readers' hearts." – Debby Giusti, Publisher's Weekly best-selling author

"**A sweet, southern stroke of brilliance**...Action, humor, mystery and a dash of romance all packed into one quirky creation. Trust me when I tell you—don't miss this one." — The Book Boost

"Reinhart's debut sparkles with wit. **A fun, fast-paced read and a rollicking start to her Cherry Tucker Mystery Series**. If you like your stories southern-fried with a side of romance, this book's for you!" — Leslie Tentler, Author of *Midnight Caller*

Books in the Cherry Tucker Southern Humorous Mystery Series:

- **A CHRISTMAS QUICK SKETCH** (prequel)
- **PORTRAIT OF A DEAD GUY**
- **STILL LIFE IN BRUNSWICK STEW**
- **HIJACK IN ABSTRACT**
- **DEATH IN PERSPECTIVE**
- **THE BODY IN THE LANDSCAPE**
- **THE VIGILANTE VIGNETTE** (Halloween novella)
- **A COMPOSITION IN MURDER**
- **A VIEW TO A CHILL,** A Maizie Albright and Cherry Tucker Interconnected Mystery
- **A MOTHERLODE OF TROUBLE,** A Cherry Tucker and Trouble the Cat interconnected story (2020)

AND MEET LARISSA'S NEWEST HEROINE

FINLEY GOODHART

"Sexy, Sassy, and Southern Suspense at its Best."

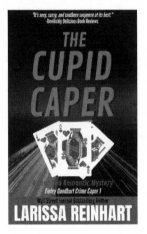

"*This is as fun a novel as it is moving and at times heart-breaking, never the more so when the final page comes and readers are only left wanting more.*"

CYNTHIA CHOW, KING'S RIVER LIFE MAGAZINE

She wants to use her criminal past to catch crooks. He wants her back. In the grift. And in his life. Can Finley Goodhart convince Lex that doing good is the greatest hustle of all?

From *Wall Street Journal* bestselling author Larissa Reinhart, the first in the Southern con artist, romantic mystery thriller, the Finley Goodhart Crime Caper series.

Ex-grifter Finley Goodhart may try to stay on the straight and narrow, but walking that thin line becomes wobbly when she believes her friend Penny was murdered. The last thing she wants is to work with her ex-partner (and ex-boyfriend), the brilliant (brilliantly frustrating) British con artist, Lex Leopold. However, when it appears Penny's demise might be related to an exclusive matchmaking service for millionaires, Fin needs Lex's help to pull a long con to get the goods on Penny.

Romance is in the air for hustlers, gangsters, and their marks. Unfortunately for Fin and Lex, infiltrating the racket doesn't make for a match made in heaven. This Valentine swindle could stop their hearts for good.

"One thing I can always count on from this author is her fabulously strong female characters. Fin doesn't disappoint and the mystery takes many twists and turns to keep a reader guessing to the very end." --Bibliophile Reviews

"Immediately engaging. Kept me guessing. Lots of surprises." --The Layaway Dragon

"Once again, Reinhart has managed to spin an intriguing tale." --Christa Reads and Writes

"This is not the first book I've read of Larissa Reinhart, and as always it **kept me glued and addicted to the story,** trying not to worry too much for our characters." --Varietats

"**Action, adventure, intrigue, intellect, and just the right amount of romance.** A great debut to a new series–I'm on the hook for more!" — Jenna C, Girl With Book Lungs

"Hang on to your hat and purse and seat as this is a wild ride. **As exciting and fast-paced as this long con is for the first half of the book, at almost exactly 50% the game plan changes!**" -- Laura's Interests

"**It's sexy, sassy, and southern suspense at its best.**" --Devilishly Delicious Book Reviews

Finley Goodhart Crime Caper series:

- **PIG'N A POKE**, a Finley Goodhart prequel (exclusive to Larissa's VIP reader group, see her website for details)
- **THE CUPID CAPER**
- TBA (2020)

ACKNOWLEDGMENTS

Ritter Ames, you're an incredible editor, book guru, and a great friend. Thank you for all the help and support.

Terri L Austin for being such an awesome critique partner and friend.

Abby Vandiver for all your hard work and effort in organizing and leading *The 12 Slays of Christmas.* Herding cats is a thankless job. You were an amazing cat herder and a lovely person.

Dru Ann Love for your continued support, encouragement, and all the great things you do for mystery writers in general. Plus for being such a sweet friend.

The Mystery Minions, know that I'm thinking about y'all while I'm writing. Thank you so much for your incredible support and friendship! Special thanks to Risa Rispoli, Susan Ray, Mina Gerhart, and Linda Burns for their medical knowledge.

And thanks to Celia Fowler, who is a wonderful woman and not married to a bank robber. Nor does she have any felons in her family. That I know of.

And to my Rockin' Review Team! You are such a huge help in each of my releases. Thanks so much for all your support.

This first appeared in *THE 12 SLAYS OF CHRISTMAS* in December 2017 with stories by Abby L Vandiver, Judith Lucci, Amy Vansant, Colleen Mooney, Amy Reade, Nell Goddin, Colleen Helme, Kim Hunt Harris, Cindy Bell, Summer Prescott, and Kathryn Dionne. A fantastic group of cozy writers and women in their own right, it was my privilege to work with them. Thank you!

And to my home posse—Trey, So, Lu, Biz—thanks for always having my six. xoxo

ABOUT THE AUTHOR

Wall Street Journal bestselling and award-winning author, Larissa Reinhart writes humorous mysteries and romantic comedies including the critically acclaimed Maizie Albright Star Detective, Cherry Tucker Mystery, and Finley Goodhart Crime Caper series. Her works have been chosen as book club picks by *Woman's World Magazine* and *Hot Mystery Reviews*.

Larissa's family and dog, Biscuit, had been living in Japan, but once again call Georgia home. See them on HGTV's *House Hunters International* "Living for the Weekend in Nagoya" episode. Visit her website, LarissaReinhart.com, and join her newsletter for a free short story.